Bloody Justice

Bloody Justice

AHMAD KALIM

StoryTerrace

Text Ahmad Kalim
Copyright © Ahmad Kalim

First print January 2023

StoryTerrace

www.StoryTerrace.com

To my family, friends and teachers, but above all, my mama.

ABOUT THE AUTHOR

I live in Berkshire with my parents and a younger sister. But I was born thousands of miles away in Karachi, Pakistan, profoundly deaf, not able to hear a single sound. I moved to the UK when I was 2, to receive better healthcare. I didn't start to speak until I was 4 and learning fluent English was only a hope.

Life was tough, to say the least, hospitals being my second home often because deafness was only a small part of my overall health challenges. That will make another book!

As a kid, I used to read a lot, as it was a key way to improve my speech and enhance my vocabulary. So after two decades of saying my first words, and everything in between, it feels surreal to have my book published!

I hope you sincerely enjoy the fruits of my labour.

Uomo Forte, Destino Forte.

Contact: Twitter via @ffsAhmad

PROLOGUE

It is a rainy but humid evening. Piano melody tenderly fills the air. Funeral attire is seen everywhere, befitting the occasion. People are gathering and whispering their condolences. Cheaply bought flowers are slowly dying. Half-eaten sandwiches are left on cracked plates. Chairs slightly screech on wooden floors as visitors take their seats to listen to the upcoming speech, expected to deliver sorrows and regrets.

Away from the conjoined living and dining room, the floor creaks as the smartly dressed lawyer gently walks to an open window next to the piano. After a moment of staring into the distance, Finn takes a sip from the silver flask that is always hidden in the inside pocket of his suit. He puts his hand softly on the shoulder of his colleague who is suffering immensely and says, 'It's time.'

She looks up and replies with pain and anger in her sparkling brown eyes, 'This is the beginning of the end.' Finn is slightly bewildered. 'What?' Jessie simply gets up and walks away to deliver the eulogy.

CHAPTER 1

A *month earlier...*

It was a sweltering hot day. The blaring sun reflected off the beautiful blue ocean. The recently refurbished Coney Island was filled with yachts and fishermen's boats. Birds were chirping cheerfully in palm trees. People were chattering away, and the loud hustle on the strip was jam-packed with restaurants and trendy shops. On the south bank of the moon-shaped island, construction was starting to gather pace on a recently bought plot of land.

Fat Craig, the owner of Turner Estates & Co., stood proudly and beamed at his workforce. 'What a beautiful day to kickstart an empire!' He then took a bite of his unhealthy-looking triple cheeseburger and said, 'I have spent buck loads on this beauty in the making. Don't fuck it up.'

'I don't want to waste my precious time sending you immigrants back to your third-world dump. Get to work!' Feeling superior, Craig threw the burger package onto the ground, even though there was a bin just ten yards away, before heading to his mini-work trailer.

About fifty meters down, hidden beneath a cluster of trees, there was an old and partially banged-up Alfa Romeo. There were two men wearing matching hoodies and ripped blue jeans. A slender and short but athletically fit brown-haired man looked in his rearview mirror. 'Lazy bastard!' Luciano

Mazzola exclaimed as he studied the land. 'Dude, you did the exact same thing an hour ago,' his older brother, Angelo Mazzola, laughed.

'Shut the fuck up and don't smoke in here, Jesus Christ! Let's move in and take out that entitled bum,' Luciano insisted.

'And then what, get rid of all the witnesses as we go along? We move at midnight.' Angelo stroked his slightly orange beard and sighed, 'I know you are using me as bait in case something goes wrong. I might not be the favourite son, but I'm smarter.'

Luciano was slightly taken aback and replied in Italian, '*Che cazzo fai qui allora?* (The fuck are you doing here then?)' Angelo responded with a devilish grin, '*E divertente.* (It is fun.)' Luciano replied calmly, 'Piece of advice, tone it down. These violent delights have violent ends.'

CHAPTER 2

It was midnight, and the air was still warm but pleasant. The land was a mess, as construction tools and materials were left all over the place. It was eerily quiet as the workers had left for the day. Fat Craig finally stumbled out of his trailer after binge-watching the latest additions to *Netflix*. He took a brisk walk, albeit with a limp, to the cliff that was overlooking the ocean, unaware that trouble was brewing. After he finished vomiting from the dodgy lunch earlier, he turned around, only to see that the Mazzola siblings were waiting patiently behind him.

On the edge of the empty land, Angelo chuckled and asked, 'Are you done?' Luciano then lifted the revolver from behind his back and remarked, 'Stella sends her regards,' before squeezing the trigger. Craig felt that time stood still as the bullet flew in slow motion. Blood splattered out onto the pavement as the fat man was knocked backwards and over the cliff into the darkness of the ocean. The ginger fella quickly dialled an acquaintance on his cell phone and simply said, '*E morto!* (He is dead!)' He hung up.

Suddenly, his face went white as a ghost as he heard a female scream. Both brothers turned around, their eyes darting in the darkness to follow the noise, and quietly said, 'Fuck!' They knew that the worst-case scenario was brewing.

CHAPTER 3

'Get her!' Angelo shouted with pure fear. He heard a bang in response as Luciano accidentally fired his gun out of shock. The siblings watched with absolute dread as the slug whizzed through the air and tore through the black fabric on the woman's chest. The victim fell as her blood began pouring out on the freshly cut grass.

Jordi was struggling to breathe as the pain washed over her body. She could not believe that her life was about to be cut short. No chance to have a family or to travel. Above all, she had wanted to grow old with her sister, Jessie. Instead, the view above faded to black and death lingered on.

The younger brother started to tremble and could only hear a high-pitched noise.

'SLAP!'

Luciano was brought back to earth by a deafening scream from his accomplice. 'What the fuck did you do?' Angelo bellowed from the bottom of his lungs. 'I meant grab her so we can talk, not fucking shoot!' The perp gazed down at the lethal weapon in his sweat-covered hand and barked back, 'I didn't mean to fire. I panicked! *Merda!* (shit!) What do we do now?'

After taking a moment to recollect himself, Angelo came up with a plan and spoke with authority. 'Get out of here. I'll take care of it.' Luciano responded with a quake in his voice, 'No, you are NOT going down for the mistake I made.' Angelo reached across and firmly grabbed his neck to bring him close and embrace him. He said restfully, '*Siamo fratelli alla morte.* (We are brothers till death.)'

'Go to the safe house and stay low. I will come when the time is right.' The distressed younger brother gave the gun to his older brother, stepped away gingerly and proceeded to leave the once empty land.

'I need to get rid of the gun and the body,' pondered the rightful heir to the crime syndicate throne. 'I love my little *fratello* (brother) but goddamn, he's not ready.'

'I told Ma, but she wouldn't listen.' He then went to the back of the car and opened the trunk to find the tarp. *No, it would be too messy, don't have the tarp to roll the body in,* Angelo thought and made another plan. The goon trotted back to the lifeless corpse and decided to pick up the victim. 'Fuck, she's heavy,' he whispered to himself. Once he had placed Jordi onto the driving seat and thrown the revolver in the river, he took the license plate off, so he could take it away and hide. He then put the car into neutral and pushed the vehicle into the sea.

CHAPTER 4

An hour ago, before the second shooting.

'Why the fuck does he not desire me?' Jessie stared intensely at the reflection of herself bouncing off the piano. She was wearing a black sleeveless tank top and green cargo pants. Jessie had dyed her hair a dirty blonde but was naturally a brunette. She continued to mutter to herself, 'I'm fit and stunning and have so much in common with Finn.'

Her finger roughly tapped the piano keys as the noise whimpered throughout the room. She raised her voice a little louder and said powerfully, 'I'll do anything to have him for myself.' 'Ahem!' Jessie turned to see her younger sister standing behind her. 'Oh, how much did you hear?'

Jordi was fiddling with her pink braid while wearing a unicorn T-shirt and black tracksuit. 'Everything,' she said. 'I'm sorry honey, but you know that's not right. Finn is engaged to a lovely woman now, you have to let it go.

Jessie rolled her eyes, embarrassed. Jordi stepped closer and gave her sister a hug. 'It wouldn't work in your profession with the rules and needing to be objective.' Silence filled the air for the next few minutes before Jessie started playing the music again.

'Why don't you meet with Jake, my maths teacher? He's smart and handsome. Go for a coffee or something,' Jordi suggested. 'Not really in the mood for dating to be honest,'

Jessie moaned. 'You need to do something to get your mind off Finn. Just come to my college and meet the nerd at recess, for God's sake,' Jordi pressed. Her older sister snapped and said, 'Zip it!'

A little while later, the younger sister suggested, 'Hey honey, let's go for a jog and get some ice cream afterwards.' Jessie looked at her watch before deciding against it as she was not in the mood.

Jordi changed into her jogging clothes and gave her older sister another warm embrace before leaving the house. Neither knew that a dark tragedy loomed ahead.

CHAPTER 5

Finn was staring at the beige ceiling with a fan hanging above him. He turned to his left side to see the time. It was seven in the morning. He flexed his arms and spotted a few empty bottles of whiskey. He remembered yesterday's victory at the court. The alcoholic groaned, 'Fuck, my head!' Finn took a look around and thought to himself that he needed a healthier way to de-stress or celebrate a win.

He turned to the table on his right and saw the missed calls on his mobile phone, all from his fiancée, Gigi. The skinny blonde with blue eyes was away visiting her parents in Boston. In order to not worry her by missing further calls, he speed-dialled 'one'.

'Hey, sunshine,' Finn said in a hoarse voice.

'About time you picked up. Late night?' his high school sweetheart responded.

'Errr, no, won the Pugh case. Well, barely.'

'You're croaking. Jesus, Finn, how many times have we talked about this?' Gigi was frustrated with the drinking, another reason why she was away. A break was needed.

To dodge the conversation that they had had many times, Finn attempted to change the subject. 'How are your parents?'

She didn't want to revisit this sensitive subject either so she went along. 'They are doing good, might move to Florida to fully enjoy their retirement.'

'That's a good idea. Oh yeah, are you feeling better? You were vomiting a few days ago.'

'Not really honey, not sure why.'

'Must be the crabs down there, innit?' Finn chuckled.

'Or maybe the mushroom pasta you cooked me last week, huh?' Gigi replied jokingly.

'Nah, my cooking is of *Michelin* standard, would win *MasterChef* easily.'

'Ah, how I've missed your cockiness.'

'That's why you went out with me in the first place, innit?'

Gigi simply smiled as she fondly remembered old times. They both said their 'love yous' before hanging up. She had a theory on why she was having morning sickness but hadn't had the time to do the all-revealing test just yet.

Finn had a quick look at his emails before deciding to take a cold shower to calm the ringing hangover.

After refreshing himself, he muttered, 'I need some food and painkillers,' and stumbled downstairs to check the couch in the living room for spare pills. He saw an open briefcase with all the case papers fallen on the floor. Kitchen? No eggs, cereal or milk. Irritated, he decided to head to the local convenience store and then the pharmacy. Just then, there was a knock on the door.

A well-built African-American police captain stood on the other side of the door, with sadness on his face. Jack Feltham said to himself, with concern in his voice, 'How the fuck am I gonna do this?' This case was going to be his and Finn's biggest test in their respective careers.

He had known Finn since childhood. They would always play sports together and cover each other's backs at school.

They both had the same dream – to serve the city of New York. As the door opened, Jack uttered a heavy sigh before taking his hat off and saying gently, 'Can I come in, please? We have a situation.'

Finn sensed a heavy calamity. He simply asked, 'One of our own? Jessie? Is she OK?' His boss shook his head and replied, 'It's her sister. Put some clothes on. We gotta notify Jessie.'

CHAPTER 6

The roar of the Mustang heightened as the chief of Brooklyn Homicide Department drove towards the south end of Coney Island. Finn broke the ice. 'What do we know so far?' The driver answered with a dry throat, 'It looks like Jordi was jogging when she stumbled upon another ongoing crime.'

'Another crime?'

'Yeah, another body was found. Some fatso.'

After another five minutes of uncomfortable silence, they reached Jessie's house. Both could hear the piano humming through an open window. The duo was dreading delivering the bad news. Jack turned the engine off and announced, 'I'll take the lead.' They both got out of the vintage but lavish vehicle, made their way and finally produced a heavy knock on the oak door.

On the other side.

Jessie was wearing a vest and cargo shorts as it was boiling hot. She heard the bump on her door and was relieved to think that her sister may be back. The detective had been worried sick all night because Jordi wasn't answering her calls. The door creaked open as both men looked at her with sadness. Suddenly, she felt sick to her stomach.

She had done these kinds of notification visits many times but never thought she would be on the receiving end of one. Her whole body and mind went numb. Her knees buckled as she tried to hold on to the radiator next to her. The visitors reacted quickly and did their best to hold her up. The effort was futile as Jessie fell to the floor in agony. She immediately passed out.

A few minutes later.

When her eyes opened, she saw both of her colleagues hovering above. She suddenly felt cold from the oak floor she fell on, even though the sun was blaring on it from a nearby window. 'Hey there, have some water,' Finn offered, with a glass in his hand. 'I'm so sorry, Jess,' Jack muttered quietly. The chief went ahead and explained what he had found out so far.

Jess quickly stood up and demanded, 'Take me to the crime scene.'

'I don't think that's a good idea,' Finn advised. The grieving sister simply repeated herself with steely determination. Jack thought about it for a second and knew his friend wouldn't let it go, so he simply bowed as they made their way to Coney Island.

CHAPTER 7

Police sirens flickered around the crime scene which was marked with yellow tapes. Reporters babbled away while cameras clicked. Patrol cops were trying to do a canvass but to no avail. As the detectives approached the ground, Finn could see the two dead bodies covered with white sheets and a wet, wrecked car. As Yuno, the medical expert, looked up, everyone else did. They all went silent for a moment before spouting condolences.

Jess didn't pay much attention as she tried to push through the crowd to identify the corpse. She bent down into a frog-like position and pulled the first sheet up. There they were, bright blue eyes, now lifeless. Jessie tried to hold back the tears. 'I'm sorry for your loss,' the Japanese American ME said. The bereaved simply nodded and asked for the COD, even though it was blatantly obvious. 'Single gunshot to the chest, with a .45 ACP calibre. TOD was at midnight.'

'Who called it in?' she asked. Jack interrupted, 'Dear, you know you can't investigate as it is too personal.' The detective roared back, 'I can't just do nothing.'

Her boss replied calmly, 'I know you are in pain, and I promise you, Finn, Jasmine and I will do our very best to get justice.' Jess knew her chief was right and reluctantly walked away. Finn and Yuno shared a moment of silence.

'Is there anything I can do for her?' Yuno enquired.

'All we can do is do our best,' Finn spoke dejectedly. 'Tell me about the second victim.'

'Well, his name is Craig Turner and the COD was the same,' replied Yuno. 'The same Craig that owns the Turner Co.?' Finn asked.

'Yup!' Jasmine, an Arab American exclaimed loudly. Everyone else was taken aback a little.

'Take it down a notch, will ya?' Finn demanded.

'Sorry.'

'Anyway, what do you know about him?' Finn went on.

The slightly embarrassed junior detective continued, 'He recently bought this land for fifteen million, and the real estate project just started yesterday.'

'The company is relatively new. How on earth could Craig afford it?' Finn wondered.

'Well, maybe his assistant, Mike, will know. He's the fella in a bright green shirt over there,' Jasmine pointed out. 'Did he call it in?' Jack asked. 'No, it was anonymous. Came from a payphone located seven blocks away. CCTV identified a person with blood stained *NY Knicks* hoodie jogging away from the scene of crime.

'Anonymous, huh? Clearly, the likely witness didn't want to stick around. They must've been scared and decided to leg it before potentially being caught by the perps,' Finn contemplated.

'Mmm, we'll have to ask the patrol cops to do the canvass but for now, let's have a quick analysis of the scene before you go and talk to Craig's assistant,' Jack commanded.

CHAPTER 8

Together, Finn and Jasmine stepped out of the crime scene and beyond the yellow tapes. They walked to the busy construction site and saw a skinny but tall man having a quick meeting with the labourers. 'Look, lads, what happened was a tragedy. But the show must go on. You are all still getting your dough. Get to work.'

'Isn't that a bit insensitive, Mr Fuller?' the lawyer asked. 'Please call me Mike. I'm sorry, but I am under huge pressure from the investors.' 'What investors?' asked Finn. 'Oh, that pasta company, Mazzola, has a seventy percent stake in the project.'

Both investigators threw a confused look at each other before Finn continued his enquiry. 'Why on earth would a pasta maker venture into real estate?'

Mike replied, 'I was curious too, but I heard that Stella Mazzola, the owner, wanted to expand her portfolio.'

'Mmm, we would expect her to be here, in that case,' Finn remarked. 'I informed her a few minutes ago, and she put me in charge on a temporary basis.'

'Just like that?' 'Yep. I have never even met her. Craig handled all of that.'

Jasmine eagerly interrupted, 'Do you know who would want to kill Craig? Where were you last midnight?' Mike was a little taken aback by the sudden burst of questioning. Finn shot him an apologetic look and gently nodded to encourage him to answer. 'Erm, well, my boss was overbearing and enjoyed his authority a little too much, but I don't think anyone would want to hurt him. I was at the bar round the corner, having a drink after a long day.'

Finn dropped in, 'Last thing, please pass on the investor's contact info, will you?' The new boss simply gave out the business card and hurried back to work. The investigative duo returned to the crime scene.

CHAPTER 9

Both the junior detective and the lawyer took an extended look around the area and the lifeless bodies. They spotted a pool of vomit with some blood mixed in it near the railings. 'Someone had an unhealthy meal of burger and chips,' Jasmine grimaced. Finn concluded, 'Yep, that was definitely Craig. We know that Jordi was jogging.'

Jack piped in and announced, 'It was an execution! He fell over the railing due to the impact of the bullet.' The lawyer noticed the powder burns on the male victim. 'The killer must have been up close when he fired the gun,' Finn confirmed. 'Jordi doesn't have any. She must have been further away.'

Jasmine turned her head and attempted to scan the area where the female victim was shot. 'Over there, there's a small puddle of blood by the tree.' She started to bag the cigarette butts and took pictures of the surrounding evidence, including boot prints and the wrecked car. They both went to the tree zone and estimated the distance. 'That's a solid ten metres from the vomit spot.'

The mood was sombre. Finn ran his hand through his hair out of nervousness and spoke up, 'She was at the wrong place at the wrong time.' The chief said with a sigh, 'Jordi was a witness.'

As that thought hit home, he took a quick look at Jessie and decided to give her company.

Jack stepped out to the bench, where his best detective was looking at her mobile. He sat down with a heavy sigh. There was tension and an uncomfortable silence in the air. Anyone could have heard a pin drop. 'Never thought I would be on the other side of pain in all my years of this bullshit,' Jess bemoaned. 'Damn, that must've hurt like hell to find out,' Jack said quietly.

'I'm sorry, Jess, but I have to ask you some questions.' Finn approached the bench and looked at her with pain in his eyes. 'I know the drill. Go on,' she replied. 'Not here. Down at the station. Finn will take you home afterwards and help with necessary arrangements,' the chief spoke softly.

The trio got up and made their way to the Mustang. Jessie took one last look at the devastation that surrounded her and thought to herself, *I'm never coming back to this shithole.*

CHAPTER 10

The engine roared as Jack started the car. He reversed out of the crime scene location and made his way to the police station. The sun was blaring, forcing everyone to roll down their windows as the heat was a bit too much. It also got rid of the strange but common musky smell that was adrift. After a long twenty minutes without a word spoken, the engine faded as they arrived at the police station, located in east Brooklyn.

Jessie was trying to hold back the tears and announced, 'Jack, I can't go in. Not with everyone looking at me.'

Her boss replied, 'I know it is extremely hard. None of us can understand the pain. But we have to follow the protocol.'

The detective snapped, 'I don't give a fuck about protocol.'

Finn was eager to defuse any potential argument and suggested, 'We can do the interview in the car. Just film it and remember to state the names and date. I'll be the witness.'

Jessie realised she was rude to her boss and apologised. 'You snapped,' Jack responded with a wry smile. The trio chuckled lightly before Finn took his mobile out. The boss took his lighter and started to smoke his cigar.

The lawyer set up the camera, held it up and started recording. 'Today is 27th of May 2020, time is 11.11 a.m. This is ADA Finn Kingsley.' He then gestured to Jack to tell him to state his name and title.

'I am Jack Feltham, chief of Brooklyn Homicide Department, and I am interviewing Jessie Knowles, the sister of the recently deceased Jordi Knowles.'

Jess gulped, and her voice croaked a little bit as she called out, 'Here.'

The interrogator continued, 'First of all, I am deeply sorry for your loss. When was the last time you spoke to her?'

'Last night before she went for a jog.'

'How did she seem?'

'OK.'

'Do you remember what time that was?'

'It was ten or fifteen minutes before midnight.'

'Why did she go for a jog so late?'

'It is too hot in the day for exercise, it was cooler then.'

'Everything was OK between you two?'

'Yes,' Jess started to cry a little. 'We had a stupid argument over my social life. I have failed her and myself. I promised our mum that I would protect her, but I failed.'

Finn interrupted, 'Jordi knew you loved her very much. This is not your fault.'

Jack suggested, 'We can do this later.'

Jess wanted to get it over with, so she signaled to continue.

The lawyer gently nodded to the chief to do so. Jack resumed, 'Do you know if anyone wanted to hurt her? Trouble at college?'

'No, she got along with everyone.'

'What about you? Any threats from perps you have put away?'

'Nothing. I would tell you if there was someone.'

'Sorry to ask you this, but where were you last night?'

Jess shot him an angry glare and responded quietly, 'At home alone. She invited me along, but I was not in the mood.'

Her boss announced, 'That'll be all. Please do let me know about any further information you might remember. Interview ended at 11.20 a.m.' He signalled Finn to stop recording.

The female detective got out of the car straight away and frantically walked, without any sense of direction.

CHAPTER 11

Finn quickly told Jack to keep him informed of any progress and revealed his plan to take her to his place for comfort. He ran after her and grabbed her arm, 'Jess, let me take you back to my place. You can make any announcements needed. I can help you.'

Jess agreed. Fifteen minutes later, they arrived at his home.

As they both stepped inside, the lawyer remembered that neither of them had eaten. He suggested he make some omelettes but soon realised he never picked up those eggs. As he tried to remember what else he had in the fridge, he noticed the gaze on him. Jess was looking at him with longing and went for a hug. Tears soaked her colleague's top. After a few moments, she attempted to kiss him in her moment of weakness.

Finn held her back firmly, 'This isn't right. You are not yourself. You need to eat something and perhaps take a nap.'

She snapped back, 'You don't know what I need!' before attempting to try again. Her colleague grabbed her hands and forcefully said, 'Jess, behave.'

Jess slumped onto a nearby couch, a bit embarrassed. Finn was shocked by the sudden development and wasn't sure how to process it. He was just glad that he had displayed self-control. Shaking his head, he proceeded to the kitchen.

After lunch, which in the end was a ready meal he took from the freezer, and a few minutes of awkward silence, Finn built up the courage to make small talk. 'So, who do you need to notify? The college and her friends?'

Jess replied flatly, 'Just the college. I never liked her friends.'

'But don't you owe it to Jordi to let her friends know?'

She dodged the question. Sensing a glare, he shook his head and got up to put the dishes away.

CHAPTER 12

'Just keep being yourself. You are doing well,' Jack advised Jasmine. She was a little down after a mini telling-off from Finn. 'It is just a stressful case. Don't take it personally.'

'Thanks, boss. I can't imagine how Jessie is feeling.'

'Me neither,' said Jack as he hit the brakes at the traffic stop. Both of them were on their way to the headquarters of Mazzola Co. It was still blazing hot and the open windows weren't helping. The duo reached a building bang in the middle of Sheepshead Bay. The general chatter brought a certain downtown liveliness to the environment. You could tell the structure was new by its sleekness. Its edges were bendy, almost like the shape of a curved penne. Some construction was still ongoing on one side.

Jasmine got out of the car and marveled, 'Damn, this must be expensive!'

Her boss quipped, 'The cost was probably all of the employees at our station combined.'

They walked inside briskly and were hit with a fresh blast of AC. 'Now I could get used to this. We need this down at the station,' the young detective exclaimed.

'We ain't got the budget,' Jack reminded her. He approached the front desk and took out his badge. 'We would like to see the CEO,' the chief requested.

'Just a moment, sir,' the keen receptionist answered before phoning the above. After a brief convo, she hung up the phone and informed the visitors, 'Stella will be down in five minutes. Please take a seat. Would you like a drink?' The guests shook their heads and sat down in the nearby waiting room.

Jack commanded, 'Let me take charge. These sneaky fucks have escaped money laundering and plenty of other charges a few times now.'

Jasmine enquired, 'Didn't you go to the same school as Stella Mazzola?'

Her boss sighed, 'Yes, she'll definitely bring it up for the hundredth time.'

'Always a charmer, eh?' Stella interrupted. The blonde with a small hint of ginger roots stood tall in her stunning red dress. Just like the old days, she would always grab everyone's attention. 'Shall we sit somewhere more comfortable?' she suggested.

CHAPTER 13

'Please come through,' Stella gestured to the investigators. Her office was located on the top floor, with a view overlooking the city. 'Here is some ice-cold water. You must both be struggling with the heat.'

Jasmine eagerly took one bottle and gulped the drink down. After taking a moment to collect herself, she thanked the CEO.

'No worries, my dear, you must have been very thirsty.'

Jack took his mobile out to record the interview and did the standard introductions.

'No pleasantries? I'm disappointed Jack,' the interviewee pouted. 'He wasn't like this when we went out you know, detective. He was full of life and took his time with me.'

The chief ignored the remarks and started the line of questioning. 'Why have you moved into real estate?'

'I was bored with making pasta. I wanted to have some fun.'

'Even though you have no experience?'

'I'm a smart gal, Jack. Have you forgotten?'

'Why didn't you visit the construction site? Isn't it important to be more hands-on after Craig died? Especially with an expensive project?'

'Nah, his newly promoted assistant has it under control.'

'Discarding the victim already?'

'Don't be so silly. It is a tragedy, but life goes on.'

'How much did you invest?'

'That's not relevant.'

'That's for me to decide.'

'Ooh, taking charge now? I like it. I invested twelve million, Craig coughed up three. I want to build the most luxurious apartments ever to exist. Would you like a slot, my dear friend?'

'No. Where were you last night, around midnight?'

'I'm insulted, Jack. You don't think I had anything to do with the murder?'

'You have the motive, Ms Mazzola.'

'And what is that?'

'Full ownership of the land and sales.'

'Don't be ridiculous, Jack. Craig had the expertise in raw materials, something I don't have.'

'Answer the question, please.'

'At the steakhouse we used to go to.' The CEO reached into her handbag and handed the receipt over. 'Had a delicious fillet. We should have dinner there one day, for old time's sake.'

'Hard pass.'

'If you say so. Can't blame a gal for trying though.'

'What about your sons?'

'They are adults. I don't always keep track of their whereabouts. You'll have to contact my lawyer if you wanna talk to them.'

'Hiding something?'

'Nah, just a mother's instinct to protect.'

'That will be all for now,' Jack said, ending the interview.

'Gotta liven up, Jack,' Stella recommended.

The mobile rang. 'Saved by the bell,' Jasmine remarked gracefully. It was getting a little intense. After a moment, Jasmine announced, 'The ME wants to see us, boss.'

'Let's go.' Jack was hugely relieved.

'We were just getting started,' Stella said with a childlike voice.

The investigators quickly said their thanks and hurried out of the door. 'She's a character, eh?' Jasmine chuckled.

'Goddamn piece of work,' Jack sighed.

CHAPTER 14

After the awkward interview, the duo were on their way back to the police station. Jasmine was curious about the aforementioned relationship, but she didn't dare to ask. Luckily, her boss spoke up.

'We were together pretty much throughout college. I left her simply because she wanted to pursue a life of crime. She wanted to be like her dad. It excited her,' Jack explained to the junior detective.

'Couldn't steer her right?' she pondered.

'Nope, and I ain't talking about this any further. It's not even 3 p.m., and I want to go home, have a drink and sleep,' the chief moaned.

As they arrived at the police station, they were met by a burst of enquiries from the press men and women, who were blocking the entrance. Both instinctively used their PR training and calmly deflected the enquiries with a default, 'No comment!'

They made their way to the basement to meet the ME. They felt an immediate coldness in the air as they entered the autopsy room.

'Those paparazzi are like vultures. No respect for the dead,' Yuno lamented. She then partially pulled the white sheets down. The corpses were both clean and ready for eye inspections.

'It's pathetic, but we have a job to do,' Jack reminded her.

'Right. The COD is obvious. Gunshot wound to the chest. I dug out a .45 ACP calibre from both victims. This matches the revolver forensics recovered from the river. TOD was at midnight.'

'Anything abnormal or foreign materials on either?'

'Nothing on either poor soul because they were submerged in water, which removed any evidence. Hopefully, the lab above will have some answers on the car or the other evidence found at the crime scene.'

'Next of kin for Craig?'

'I have notified his daughter. She will be coming in a bit to confirm the identity.'

'When can Jessie bury Jordi?'

'She can come and collect the body in a couple of days.'

'I will let her know in a bit.'

'How is she doing? Must be so difficult. It was just them two in the family, right?'

'Yeah, their mum passed away a year ago. All we can do is our very best to bring justice,' the chief encouraged both ladies.

'In fact, I am going to head over to Finn's to update them both. Jasmine, please write up what we know so far and establish the timeline on the whiteboard. Call me when the lab has something.'

CHAPTER 15

The east of Brooklyn was mostly quiet, filled with empty buildings, apart from one very busy warehouse. It was buzzing with delivery drivers loading their vans with pasta when a limo turned up. 'Thank you, I won't be long,' Stella said to her chauffeur before stepping out of the vehicle. She made her way to the back of the building, where the office was located.

A chime rang as Stella walked through the office door. She saw the two boys, both looking dejected. Stella immediately cupped Luciano's cheeks and asked eagerly, 'Oh, my *bambino*, are you OK?'

'Yes ma. I'm not a child!' the younger son said, slightly annoyed at the pampering.

'You will always be my baby,' his mum responded.

Angelo cleared his throat and announced, 'I am OK as well, you know.'

Stella berated him, 'You had one job. Remove Craig and any trace of you being there.'

The eldest son snapped back, 'I told you he wasn't ready! I had to stage the crime scene to make it look like an accident. Luca couldn't even handle a gun!'

'You should've taken the weapon away from him in the first place. He was supposed to be the getaway driver!' Stella exclaimed.

Luca tried to butt in and said meekly, 'Ma, it ain't his fault. I was trying too hard.'

'Don't worry my bambino, all will be OK,' his mum responded.

'This is the thanks I get?' Angelo roared. 'Fuck this, I'm outta here!'

Stella collected her breath and apologised, 'I'm sorry, *miele* (honey), my bad, did you clear away any potential evidence?'

The eldest son also calmed down and replied, 'Yes, I also pushed the car in the water, as if the vehicle went off the road and the witness was a driver, crashing into Craig.'

'Ah, to look like an accident. You are smarter than I give you credit for!' Mama admitted.

'Don't talk to anyone. Just work here and stay low, both of you.'

The little brother asked, 'But what about the cops?'

'Just ask your sister Ilara to accompany you if they approach either one of you. I will update her. After all, she is a successful defence attorney. I'll take care of the rest.'

Both brothers looked at each other and felt calm for the first time since the incident. 'Let's get back to work. These pasta ain't gonna deliver themselves.'

CHAPTER 16

The weather was getting unbearably hot. The chief decided to make a quick stop at his house to change into something more comfortable. He arrived at the entrance of his luxurious four-bedroom bungalow in Bay Ridge and rang the intercom. 'Jamie, it's me. Open the gates, please.'

The security guard suddenly woke up from his mini nap and scrambled to let the driver in. 'Sorry boss. The heat is getting to me,' Jamie muttered quickly in embarrassment.

Jack sighed heavily and said, almost holding his tongue. 'No worries. Drink some water and try to stay awake, please.' 'Useless shit!' he murmured softly. The giant sentry thankfully didn't hear him, as he was a hothead and would have crushed him easily.

Today had been a terrible day thus far, but the commander of BHD was grateful for the top quality of life he had worked hard for. The mini-mansion contained a swimming pool, games room with a cinema embedded, jacuzzi tub, sauna, en-suite bathrooms for each sleeping space, marble floors all around and a high-end designer kitchen.

Even with all that, there was something missing. A partner? No, he relished being a single parent. He couldn't figure out what the void was inside him. But this was no time to ponder.

'Hey Dad, you're home early. Everything OK?' Grace, his eldest kid asked.

'Shit day at the office. Jessie's sister was murdered,' Jack muttered while embracing her.

'Oh my God, how?'

'Wrong place, wrong time.'

'Where is she? I would like to go and give my condolences.'

'Best to give her some space. She has Finn with her for now.'

'And that's a good thing?'

'What do you mean?'

'You know that she has a thing for Finn?'

'Don't be silly. He is very professional. I have to quickly change and go over there to update them both.'

'Sure you don't need me to come?'

'No, honey, I'll manage. Make sure Liz does her homework, please.'

'Of course Papa!'

He ran upstairs and ditched the standard uniform to change into summer clothes, a white T-shirt and brown khakis. Five minutes later, he was on his way with a fresh batch of cigars in his shirt pocket. Jack lit one as he drove out of the gate.

CHAPTER 17

For the second time that day, Jack arrived at Finn's, also in Bay Ridge. The light attire barely helped combat the heat. Before he had a chance to knock, Finn opened the door.

The smell of coffee filled the air as the chief walked in. He also saw the empty bottles lying around the place. 'Bro, you need to work on your habit. I am surprised your liver has lasted this long,' Jack suggested for the hundredth time. 'I don't want to be visiting you in a hospital next time, or worse, a grave.'

Finn stared back with intensity and said firmly, 'I'm fine.'

If there weren't more pressing matters, Jack would've dragged him to the nearest AA. He held his tongue and made his way through to the living room.

'Thank you, and yes, please send her things home Miss Wilson,' Jessie requested before hanging up. 'Too stuck up her own ass for a school principal,' she moaned, unaware that both of her colleagues were just behind her.

The lawyer cleared his throat.

'Ah, boss, didn't know you were here. You know what, I'm not sorry you heard that,' Jess said flatly.

Jack sighed and asked Finn for a cup of coffee. 'Hey darling, how are you doing?' He immediately regretted his attempt at small talk.

The detective avoided the pity emitting from her boss and got straight to the point. 'What's the latest? Who owns the land? There was another body?'

'It's an ongoing investigation. You know very well I can't reveal the specifics.'

'I'm going mad here, doing fuck all!' she yelled back.

'Jess, chill!' he commanded.

Finn saw the tension rising and put his drink down in order to intervene. 'Guys, calm! Jack, let her work from here. She can pass on questions or whatnots to you or Jasmine. Nobody else has to know.'

His childhood friend recollected himself for a moment and had a think. He then decided, 'I'll update you on the case, but you cannot get involved under any circumstances.'

'But —'

'No buts,' Jack put his foot down.

'Fine!'

Relieved, the chief sat down and brought them both up to date. After half an hour, his phone rang. 'OK sir, I'm on my way.'

'Who was that?' Jessie probed.

'The mayor. He wants to know what's going on. I have to hold a press conference as well. I gotta go. Promise you'll behave.'

'When can I collect the body?' she asked while holding back the tears. Felt like each time she sobbed, it was a waterfall.

'Soon,' he replied dimly. He motioned Finn to walk him to the door.

'Go easy on her Jack, she's hurting.'

'I am leaving her with you. Keep an eye on her please, and that'll require you to stop drinking,' he ordered before leaving.

CHAPTER 18

Jessie waited for the loud engine noise to fade away before turning to Finn once again, as he came back to the sofa. 'Fuck him. He thinks he's superior cos he has a fancy ass hat and a ranking medal,' Jessie poured out. 'Finn, let us work on this together. You know we are better as a team than anyone else.'

'The best?'

'Of course. Remember when we were five years old and Jack lost his bike, but we found it?'

'Yeah, haha.'

'Prick didn't even thank us. Went to his momma and claimed he found it himself.'

'It wasn't that big of a deal.'

'Or what about when he stole dollars from the bike store when we were fourteen?'

'He had just lost his dad. It was an outlet.'

'Or when he stole your girlfriend Stella at high school, only to dump her a year later?'

'Blessing in disguise to be honest. She's a nutcase.'

'What about the first case we all did together? We did most of the work, only for him to swoop in at the end and make himself look like a hero?'

'J—'

Jessie got up and barked, 'Why the fuck are you defending him?'

'I'm just trying to be fair.'

'Bullshit!'

After a few minutes of uncomfortable silence, Finn settled to take a gamble. 'Look, there's a whiteboard in my room. Take it to the guest space and do your work there. I'll say it was me brainstorming solo.'

Jessie was relieved to have some good news at last. 'Thank you, Finn. I knew I could count on you,' she said before exiting the living room to start contemplating.

'Don't make me regret it,' he shouted after her. 'Fuck, I need another drink,' he groaned. The lawyer got up and searched three different cabinets, to find only a half-drunk whiskey flask. 'Eh, good enough,' he whispered to himself before taking a heavy gulp.

CHAPTER 19

'Settle down!' Judge Taylor ordered the crowd in the courtroom as the bailiff handed him the jury's verdict. He took a quick look before turning to the panel filled with ordinary humans. They were all sweating profusely but relieved that the proceedings were coming to a close. It had been a long trial, especially in the current weather.

'On the count of property fraud, what say you?'

'We find the defendant, not guilty,' the forewoman of the group announced.

Loud cheers erupted from the defence side. Rage and bombarding questions broke out from the prosecution bench. The judge had to bang his gavel to gain attention and warned, 'Any more noise from anyone, they will be charged with contempt of court!'

He went on with the rest of the court process before ending the trial. People started to filter out, followed by grumblings and cameras flashing.

The client quickly hugged and thanked the defender before departing to enjoy his freedom (and probably get into trouble again in the near future).

'Another one for the books!' Joanne said excitedly. Her boss, Ilara, simply nodded. She was dark-skinned with brown hair and green eyes. 'Aren't you happy?' her assistant enquired.

'Eh, another day, another dollar,' she replied flatly.

'Big bonus, though. Don't you want to take a holiday to the Bahamas or somewhere exotic?' Jo was too eager for a celebration. After all, she loved to party and wake up the next day with no memory of what happened the previous night.

'What about some time for us?' Jo said cheekily. They had been dating in secret for a couple of years.

'Lower your voice,' her boss whispered abruptly.

'Embarrassed by me?' her lover pouted.

'No, you know that's not true. It's just I can't go anywhere. My family is always needing me for something or the other. My brothers are idiots.'

'Speaking of close ones . . .' Jo murmured and pointed behind.

Ilara looked at her and spun around. Her mother, Stella, was standing at the door in her usual bright outfit.

'Ah, shit, here we go again.' A quick exchange of pleasantries was followed by a swift exit from the courthouse.

CHAPTER 20

After some bumping and pushing through a crowd of paparazzi, the trio reached the limo, only for Stella to stop at the curb. She gazed at Ilara, signalling that the forthcoming conversation was to be private.

Ilara was annoyed at the suggestion and said, '*Veramente?* (Really?)'

Her mum did not like the disrespectful tone. She couldn't risk telling her off in front of everyone as a public argument would ensue. Holding her tongue, she simply nodded and motioned her to get into the vehicle quickly.

Ilara shot a sympathetic look at Joanne and mouthed 'sorry' before ducking inside. She didn't have time or energy to explain her current personal life to her mum.

Mother and daughter settled into the lavish limousine. It contained every perk one could think of. A fully stocked mini-bar, a small TV with premium cable, massage chairs and imported cigars.

The attorney was once again taken aback by the luxury. After a few minutes of peace had passed, she broke the ice, 'Shoot!'

'Honey, let's catch up first. How is Johnny treating you?' Stella was always interfering in her personal life. She was so invasive that Ilara had made up a boyfriend to satisfy her curiosity, too scared to reveal her bisexuality.

She dodged the question and immediately got straight to the point. 'Get over with the pleasantries. What did the boys do now?'

'Ah, there's more to life than work, *miele*!' she said while looking out of the window. She had always loved witnessing the buzz in New York City. After another few moments of awkward silence, she announced, 'They fucked up again.'

She went on to explain the last forty-eight hours but was stopped abruptly by her only daughter. Ilara was furious to be dragged into family troubles again. 'You know I can have my licence revoked! Why can't you lot just be honest? It would be a lot easier if I just turned you all in and got on with my life!'

Stella avoided the truth and manipulated her for the thousandth time. 'You'll do the right thing for us once again, fighting for the family.'

Her daughter looked away in shame and wondered about running away and starting afresh with her real lover. But then, she always circled back to her mantra. Blood is thicker than water, but family isn't just about blood.

CHAPTER 21

Multiple flashes from the cameras and bubbles of noise emitting from hungry journalists ensued as Jack arrived at the front of the press conference, with some members of his team in the background.

Along with notifying the next of kin of victims, he also hated this part of the job. He didn't like the deceased's life coming to light and the nosy interruption to the investigation. Nonetheless, he drank some water before getting to it.

He looked at the crowd before choosing the reporter from the local news to begin the questioning.

'Can you tell us how Mr Turner died?'

'Gunshot wound to the chest.'

'Which weapon was used?'

'There are certain parts of the investigation we won't be revealing, per policy.'

He moved on to the next correspondent.

'Is it true that Mazzola Co. has a stake in the new development?'

'No comment.'

'Didn't you and ADA Kingsley have a part in their recent acquittal with the drug charges? Are you making it a personal mission to go after the pasta makers?'

'We are not going after anybody, and I'm sure everyone knows the public details of the recent land deal. We will explore each piece of evidence thoroughly and follow the path where it takes us.'

Five minutes in, and Jack was already exhausted with the enquiries. He decided to answer one more before ending the gathering. He pointed at the reporter hailing from the national cable news network.

'Is it true that there was a second body named Jordi Knowles, someone close to Detective Jessie Knowles?'

The chief of BHD was shocked at the revealing line of enquiry. This information was not made public. He realised that there was a leak within the department and stormed off.

Thomas, or Tom, the PR manager, apologised for the sudden abrupt ending of the press conference and ran after Jack. He caught up to him, and even before he could say anything, the chief ordered him to personally meet the last journalist. The scared fellow simply obliged.

CHAPTER 22

As Tom went to fulfil his boss's wishes, Jack realised he needed to cool down and be diplomatic with the reporter. He looked around and saw a water cooler. 'Perfect,' he muttered to himself before grabbing a plastic cup and drinking some more cold water.

Back in the media room, Tom scanned the group before spotting the requested journalist. He brushed through a sweaty group of people before tapping on the shoulder of the person he found. The pink-haired woman spun around and asked, 'Oh, am I getting an exclusive?'

'Yes, an exclusive telling-off.'

'Ohh, I might get a spanking.'

'Behave Audrey, please.' Tom was embarrassed. He ushered her into the quiet conference room.

'Honey, don't be jealous. He may have picked me but I'm all yours. The secret is safe with me. See you tonight!' Audrey said lovingly. She quickly kissed the PR manager before entering the squared space. As the door opened, Jack uttered a huge sigh, in an effort to stay calm. 'Nice to meet you,' he said, as he put his hand out for a handshake.

'Audrey,' she replied and shook his hand.

'Please sit.'

'I'm good. This won't take long, I presume.'

The commander sighed again before taking another sip of cold water. He got straight to the point. 'For the sake of the victims and the investigation, who is your source?'

'Pardon?'

'How did you know about the second fatality?'

'Ah, I can't reveal my sources. You know, source confidentiality laws.'

'But what about the casualties? And the people who are grieving? Do you want to tell them that you have compromised the investigation for justice?'

'Relax. It's not like I revealed the actual details of the murder.'

'I can take you to court for obstruction of justice.'

'No, you won't! I have better things to do, and I'm pretty sure you and your team have the necessary abilities to solve the case. May I leave?'

Jack knew he had no chance. He simply nodded. After the reporter left the room, he threw the cup across the room and kicked the chair. He took a moment to collect himself before calling Tom in.

CHAPTER 23

As soon as Tom came in, Jack got into his face and pointed at his chest. 'It was you, wasn't it?' the chief accused the department's PR manager sternly.

'Huh?' The suspected mole was shocked. It didn't take long for his boss to figure it out. He was going to try his best to defend himself.

'I've seen the chemistry you have with Audrey. Don't bullshit me.'

Tom gave in and meekly admitted, 'I'm sorry, but she just got this new prestigious job, and she is already under tough scrutiny. She needed juice to make an impression.'

'She needed juice? And what about the victims and the integrity of the investigation?' Jack roared. A tense and awkward moment followed. The commander looked out of the window and tried to think of his next step.

'All right, you will be suspended without pay temporarily. Probably for a couple of weeks.'

'But —'

'Shut the fuck up. You are lucky to still have a job.'

'Who else is going to help you with PR matters?'

'I can handle them myself for a bit. Get out of here. Fucking beta male.'

Tom felt extremely annoyed with himself. He should have known better.

Jack knew he had to phone the team about the incident. He quickly made the calls to Jasmine and Finn. Along with informing them that Tom wasn't part of the team in the coming days, he also ordered them to not have any contact with him.

He suddenly remembered that Liz, his youngest daughter, would be on her way home from school. He phoned the elder, Grace.

'Honey, is Liz home yet?'

'Any minute now. Are you coming soon?'

'I don't know. Make sure she eats her food and does her homework.'

'Of course. You worry too much.'

'I do, eh? OK, I will text you when I am on my way, whenever that might be.'

'Bye. Love you.'

'Me too, and give my love to Liz as well, please.' He hung up and then proceeded to light his cigar. It was his coping mechanism.

CHAPTER 24

It was a warm but pleasant early evening at the luxury complex located in Sag Harbour, a village embedded in Long Island. This particular house cost the criminal family eleven million. The stunning building featured five bedrooms, four bathrooms, a games room, a cinema, living room, dining room, maid's quarters and a kitchen.

The theme was over-the-top marble finishing, mostly white with some dark tones. The best bit? A huge garden complete with a stunning view and access to the waterfront, with a reserved dock in place. All of it was protected by sentinels in savvy suits.

'It's family time,' Stella boasted as she and her daughter entered the family home and stood in the grand hallway. Ilara grew up here but now had a place of her own in the city. Most of the memories here were pleasing, but she didn't like the extravagant lifestyle her mother and brothers currently lived. Being a lawyer and defending hundreds of low-class clients had changed her outlook on the rich and poor contrast.

'*Cameriera, dove sei?* (Maid, where are you?)' No response. Stella was already impatient. She yelled once again, and this time, Gina answered, '*Si, Signora?* (Yes, Madam?)'

The donna gave her the jacket, scarf, glasses and bags for her to put away and nudged her daughter to do the same. '*È pronta la cena?* (Is the dinner ready?)' she asked. The help, who could barely hold all the items, replied, '*Cinque minuti,*

Signora. (Five minutes, Madam)' Italian was obviously her first language as she hailed from Naples.

'Ma, take it easy on her!' Ilara insisted. She was often annoyed by how her mum treated the servant.

'Easy bella, she's fine. Let's go outside and wait for your brothers,' Stella uttered ignored her daughter's concern.

The duo walked out and felt their feet brush against freshly cut grass. They reached the shore and picked up much-desired glasses of wine. These were prepared shortly beforehand. The sun was shining, and there was a gentle breeze. Both were enjoying the peace that the waterfront had to offer before being interrupted.

'Hey Ma! I missed you!' Luciano hollered and hugged his mother tightly.

'*Piccolo!*' Stella was equally enthusiastic to see her youngest son.

'Jesus Christ, it has only been a few hours since you left the warehouse,' the eldest child spoke up. He shook his head at both his mother and brother before greeting his sister. 'You're good?'

'Yes.'

'Congrats on the case.'

'And to you for getting into trouble again.'

'*Per l'amor del cazzo* (For fuck's sake), can't you just be happy and chill for once?' the orange-haired male raised his voice along with the usual Italian hand gestures.

'No, I can't, because it will be me who will be asked to bail you out once again,' she roared back. Ilara and Angelo never saw eye to eye since he got deeply involved in the day-to-day activities of the crime syndicate.

'*Bambini, calmatevi!* (Children, calm down!),' said Stella, nagging at them. She hated when her kids fought. But this was bound to happen as the siblings were in a conflict of interest due to their respective 'occupations'.

'Guys, it's a nice day. We should feel blessed that we are together and healthy. Let's just enjoy the moments,' Luciano reminded both siblings as he put his arms around their shoulders. They didn't reply.

'That's right, *piccolo!*' his mum chuckled. Finally, Gina brought plates of delicious-looking food to the round wooden table. What was on the menu? Freshly caught lobsters, which had been butter poached, caviar, chips, a couple of dips, focaccias and seafood linguini. '*Grazie,* Gina,' all of them said in unison, before diving in to devour the feast.

CHAPTER 25

It was a brand new day. The sun shone through the windows, illuminating the detective. Markings on the whiteboard, papers on the floor, empty coffee cups on the side table. Jessie was lying on the guest bed, trying to gather and calm her thoughts. She closed her eyes and had the first of many flashbacks.

'Ten, nine, eight, seven,' Finn started to count down. The girls giggled and ran away to hide. Jessie spotted a small square door on the ceiling, which led to the attic. She and Jordi pulled down the stepladder quietly and proceeded to climb. Once they reached the top, the younger sister hid in the chest box, where the portable piano was stored. Her sister took cover behind a pile of boxes and covered it with a blanket.

They were both relishing this classic game, perhaps a little too much, as Jordi chortled and accidentally stepped on one of the high pitch piano keys. The girls had forgotten to close the door behind them, enabling the sound to ring throughout the second floor. Soon after, Finn found them, and they all fell laughing onto the wooden floor.

Jessie opened her eyes as a male voice brought her back to the hear and now, 'J, are you asleep?'

'No Finn, just had a small dream about Jo.' Tears started to stream down her face once again. The lawyer looked at her with compassion but had no idea how to support his grieving colleague.

'What was the dream about?'

'Hide and seek, the time when Jo stepped on the piano.' They both chuckled softly. Finn had a light-bulb moment. 'Be right back,' he said eagerly as he turned away.

'Huh?' Jessie looked up only to see him gone. After a moment, she heard footsteps grow louder as he came back into the room.

Her eyes lit up as she saw the same portable piano that appeared in her flashback. 'Really, dude?'

'Yep, thought you might need a break from the case. Think of it as a mindfulness tune,' he explained and set down the portable version of the instrument.

The detective quickly got up and excitedly hugged Finn. It was a thoughtful gesture. She then sat down on the bed and proceeded to play some soothing music. Finn went to get the case files and a hot drink. He returned soon and sat next to her, listening and working.

CHAPTER 26

A few hours of music, casework and lunch passed by. Jessie kept staring at the picture of Jordi. She was deep in thought, wondering about the new construction site. 'Who owns the fucking land?' mumbled the detective.

'Mazzola Co. does,' Finn answered.

'Ah, didn't realise you were listening.'

'Well, I've been watching you for the past couple of hours. You look exhausted, go to sleep.'

'Hang on, let me complete the timeline.'

'Jess . . .'

'Yeah, yeah, I will soon. Let me focus, please.'

The lawyer sighed. He took a big sip of whiskey before getting up and standing next to Jessie. 'You know, Craig raised a few eyebrows by partnering with Stella for this project.'

'How much did they invest into this? What was the split?'

'At least fifteen million. I think the Mazzolas put in like twelve but will only get thirty percent of the profit.'

'That seems like a shitty deal. Why do it?'

'I think because Craig has contacts in construction and real estate. Also, easier access to permits.'

'Both were killed at midnight,' Jessie said while trying to hold back tears.

'J . . .'

'I'm OK, give me a drink,' she demanded.

Finn obliged before continuing. 'The perps tried to stage the scene, but we found inconsistencies everywhere.'

'Anything from the lab?'

'No.'

'Bullet calibre?'

'.45 ACP casings were found, coming from a *Smith & Wesson* revolver.'

'Not helpful, that's a common revolver.'

'We are analysing the bullets.'

'Who found the bodies?'

'It was an anonymous phone call.'

'What about Craig's assistant?'

'Checking his alibi and financials.'

'Is he a suspect?'

'Don't think so. He seems a submissive type who wouldn't have anything to gain from the murder.'

'Any witnesses?'

'Canvass still ongoing.'

Jessie sighed and sat down on the bed. She then took off her top, now only wearing an almost see-through vest and pants. 'Sleep with me. I don't want to be alone.'

'I don't think it's a good idea.'

'Come on, I'll behave. I just need a cuddle. Do it as friends.'

'Ermmm . . .'

'Why are you being like this?'

'You know I am engaged to Gigi.'

He rapidly left the room to avoid any more awkwardness. Jessie sobbed herself to sleep as the emotional trauma of the past few days got a bit too much.

CHAPTER 27

Cheap hot drinks and stale bagels and doughnuts occupied the squad room at the police precinct. Away from the space full of old, lazy detectives, there was a gathering of motivated investigators hustling in the conference area. Jasmine looked proudly at the whiteboard, neatly arranged.

Reminders were on one side, post-it notes on the opposite. A timeline had been created, but there wasn't much on it, just the time of death and when the bodies were found. On a separate whiteboard, victims' profiles and information about the aforementioned construction deal were splattered across the panel.

As Jack walked in, everyone stood up and greeted him as if he was royalty. The chief got to the point straight away. 'What's the latest?' He moved around a couple of things on the board, a weak attempt at making any sort of connection.

'Still waiting on the result of the cigarettes and boot prints found at the scene. The wrecked car just arrived at the examining garage. The blood belonged to Jordi.'

'Canvass?'

'A dog walker bumped into a hooded man at one of the Coney Island exits. They had a dark fresh stain on their *NY Knicks model 2000*, left shoulder region. It was too dark to make him or her out.'

'No one saw the car being pushed into the water?'

'Unfortunately not.'

'Fuck's sake. Financials?'

'Nothing abnormal.'

'Tell the lab to put a rush on the evidence. We owe it to Jessie to find the perp swiftly.'

'And Craig,' Jasmine reminded him. The young detective then opened her mobile to phone the lab.

'Yeah, yeah,' Jack muttered, as if he didn't really care too much about the main victim. He encouraged everyone in the room to work harder before leaving. Back in his office, he shut the blinds, indicating to his staff not to bother him as he wanted some peace.

CHAPTER 28

It had been a couple of days. Things were moving slowly with the case. Finn decided to pop into the police precinct. He notified Jessie of his intentions but knew that she'd want to tag along.

'Let me come. I want to see where the team is at with the case. A bit of fresh air would be good,' Jessie requested.

'Fresh air, by going to the police station? Get outta here J. Go for a walk alongside the Brooklyn bridge.'

'But —'

'No buts. I advise you to not interfere under any circumstances. Hell, you shouldn't be working in the guest room even.'

'Finn, things are too slow. Let me go and get the investigation moving.'

'Don't push my buttons. Do you want me to lock you in like a pet?' the lawyer raised his tone.

'No . . .'

Finn realised he was a little harsh. He gave her a quick hug and apologised. He then suggested, 'Why don't you cook something or read a book? Get your mind off the case. I'll try not to be long.'

He left the house to drive in his old 1969 Dodge Charger. It had belonged to his grandfather, who gifted it to him before he passed away. After fifteen minutes, he arrived at the station. He took a quick gulp of alcohol before heading inside.

After the routine security checks at the entrance, the lawyer took the lazy route via the lift. The doors creaked open as he walked through into the squad room. He did not find any updates on the case in there. He left and as he strolled through the place, he gave his usual greetings to those he worked with on a regular basis.

Dud dud dud! Finn knocked.

Jack knew it was his friend due to the distinctive tapping on the door. He sighed heavily and invited him in. 'Before you ask, shit is still slow.'

'I know. Just checking in. How are you doing?'

'Knackered. Media and bosses are both on my ass. Tossers are forgetting that forensics move like a snail.'

'Same old song, I see.'

'Yep. How is Jess?'

'She's struggling, as expected.'

Jack got up from his leather chair, walked over to the window and looked out. The city of Brooklyn was full of life, hustling and bustling. After a moment of admiration, he wondered, 'Not getting involved in the investigation, I hope?'

'No,' Finn lied.

'Good. You know our purpose in life is to protect and serve the people of New York. We can't fail one of our own.'

'I agree. If we don't maintain justice, darkness will consume us.'

'Ayo, don't get poetic with me,' Jack bemoaned. But before he could continue, Jasmine popped her head in the doorway and asked if it was a good time to interrupt.

'You already did,' both men said in unison. Her boss motioned her to come in.

CHAPTER 29

Jasmine walked in, twitching a little, which was an indication of nerves. Sort of mumbling, she announced, 'We have the results from the cigarettes found at the scene,' and paused.

'Are you expecting a drum roll, detective?' Jack spoke sarcastically. He was losing his patience. She cleared her throat and came right out with it. 'There's a familial match with you boss.'

A combination of shock and befuddlement was afoot in the office. 'Huh?' said Finn. He put his hand out, wanting to see the details of the DNA report. After a quick glance, he confirmed it. Jack was in disbelief and had to sit down to compose himself.

'This can't be. My daughters were at home with me when the crime occurred,' he said.

'Your girls are obviously not involved – it's a male match. Could you have a son you don't know of?' Finn tried to make sense of this extraordinary news.

Jack had a sudden thought, which led him to exit the office in a rush and without another word. Both the lawyer and junior detective called out after him but received no reply. Finn asked Jasmine to keep it down low for now before quickly dashing to catch up with the chief. As he ran out to the parking lot, Jack had already left.

A few minutes later and some blocks away, Jack entered a pharmacy and quickly picked up a DNA kit. He ignored greetings from the shopkeeper as he clearly had a lot on his mind. His mobile phone rang a few times on his way over there and did once again. He had a quick peek at the caller ID in case it was one of his kids, but it was Finn. He ignored the call, paid the bill and left the drugstore, all within five minutes. Before setting off, he texted Stella to meet him at their spot, now!

CHAPTER 30

Jack rushed through the Bush Terminal Park, located at the north of Bay Ridge. These particular grounds had breathtaking views of the waterfront and the scenic Manhattan skyline on the other side. The chief had fond memories, mainly from his high school times. As he reached the end, he let out a heavy sigh and leaned against the railings as he looked out to the river.

He was waiting for Stella. After a few minutes passed, he saw a canoe. He chuckled and remembered a particular trip from some summers ago.

'That was a beautiful time in my life. We had our first kiss right there,' Stella piped up as she arrived.

'I remember,' Jack spoke tenderly.

'Followed by heartache a year later, at this very spot,' Stella remarked sadly.

He didn't reply as they had gone through this a few times in the past. There was a more pressing matter plaguing his mind. *No more delay, just come out with it*, he thought.

'Is one of your children related to me?' He went straight for it.

'I knew this day would come,' she said, starting to choke a little.

'Huh?'

'You see, when you asked me to come here on the very night of the break-up, I was pregnant.'

'What? How far along were you? Why didn't you tell me?' Jack raised his voice as he felt angry and hurt.

'You made it clear that you didn't want anything to do with me from that point onwards!' she snapped back.

Both stayed silent for a few minutes to collect themselves. Stella then gave Jack the toothbrush for DNA testing.

'Whose?' he enquired.

'Angelo's.'

'Won't he notice that it's missing?'

'Already replaced.'

The chief proceeded to do a quick test, and the result was positive.

Jack was overwhelmed with emotions and felt his identity was finally complete with the blood bond. Even though his two daughters were very dear to him, he had always wanted a boy. Someone to play catch with, take fishing or have a cold beer with after a long day of work. If only Stella had told him then, life would have turned out very differently.

'Hot damn, I would've stayed with you if I knew, bella.'

'You haven't called me that in ages. I miss you, *amore*.'

'I have to go and take this to the lab,' Jack said dejectedly before leaving. He threw the kit in the trash but kept the toothbrush, which was wrapped in tissue to temporarily preserve the DNA. Stella watched him go, still reminiscing quietly about old times.

CHAPTER 31

'It's mad that you had a son all these years, and you didn't know,' Finn said, shocked. Both childhood friends were smoking cigars on the high-level terrace at the police station.

'It IS mad,' Jack agreed.

'Life would have been very different if you had stayed with Stella.'

'I would have been a damn criminal. Her father wanted me to be part of the crime syndicate. He thought I had the talent to take his unsavoury business international.'

'I remember. Interesting fella. Heard he died of a heart attack a few years ago.'

'No shit. He was fatter than the piano Jess plays.'

Both chuckled in unison before recollecting high school. While they were debating about the basketball team they both once were a part of, they were interrupted by Jasmine.

'Boss, can I speak please?'

Both men put their cigars down in the mini ashtray before Jack answered her. 'You may.'

The junior detective once again stuttered, announcing, 'Angelo Mazzola is a familial match to you, boss.'

No one spoke for some time. Birds chirping on a nearby tree seemed to bring a little bit of tranquility as Jack planned his next move. He finally decided. 'Can you both pay Angelo a visit? Ask him to come to the station, please?'

Both simply nodded and got on their way. As they entered the lift, they discussed where the suspect could be. 'I guess we will be visiting the headquarters of the company?' Jasmine assumed.

'No, let's visit one of their warehouses, catch them by surprise.'

'Which one? They have many.'

'Let's go to the flagship location, located in the very east of Brooklyn.' Both settled with the idea as they exited the station.

CHAPTER 32

Finn and Jasmine arrived at the busy stockroom, wanting to talk to Angelo Mazzola but intending to keep a low profile. Finn noticed his colleague was giving off cop vibes, with a badge visible from her belt buckle and her body language. 'At least hide the badge,' Finn bemoaned. He went ahead while Jasmine fiddled with her belt clip before apologising and then following him inside.

The workers started to taunt and whistle, as they weren't fans of law enforcement, but quietened down when Ilara came out from the office to investigate the commotion.

'Back to work, fellas. How can I help Brooklyn's finest? Ah, Finn Kingsley, we meet again,' she welcomed them.

'Unfortunately, yes we do.'

'Why so grim? Still drinking?'

Finn dodged the subject and asked if he could speak to Angelo. Before she could reply, the ginger-haired male appeared and asked, '*Sorella* (sister), is he troubling you?'

'No.'

Just then, Luciano also came out on hearing the commotion but stayed silent, being nervous at the sight of the unannounced visitors.

Jasmine spotted a *NY Knicks* hoodie hanging in the office through an open door and nudged Finn. He looked that way thoughtfully, considering a potential piece of evidence. The female lawyer followed their gaze and realised what they were observing.

In anticipation, Ilara stepped ahead and closed the office door. She said sternly, 'This is private property. We let you in as a courtesy, but you can't snoop around.'

Both brothers jeered at the duo, but their sister told them to shut up, which they did.

Jasmine attempted to be bold and warned all three, 'Are you interfering with an investigation? Not a good look, is it?'

Finn held her back gently and reminded her, 'We don't have probable grounds to search the area. Let's just continue the conversation down at the station.'

The female lawyer agreed. 'Young detective, you should listen to Finn. He's a remarkable adversary. Anyway, yes no problem. We will come down tomorrow as it is getting a little late now. We have to gather our thoughts as well.'

'All right then. 1 p.m.?'

Ilara looked at both brothers, who signalled that the time was fine. 'See you then,' she remarked. Unexpectedly, the phone rang. Everyone checked their pockets, only for Finn to realise that it was his. He excused himself and went to a quiet corner. 'Is it urgent, honey?'

'Yes, it can't wait,' Gigi said on the other side.

'What's the matter? Did something happen to your parents?'

'No! I am pregnant Finn!'

'What? Really? We're having a family?'

'We ARE, honey!'

'That's amazing! I have to go now, but we have to start thinking of names ASAP!'

Both giggled and said their 'love yous' and goodbyes. Awkwardly, since the lawyer had been loud with excitement, the whole warehouse had heard the good news.

'Congratulations are in order Mr Kingsley,' Ilara said politely. Others applauded, out of social manners rather than real affection.

'Thanks,' Finn replied sheepishly before both he and Jasmine left the warehouse. The lawyer headed home, while Jasmine made her way to the station to update Jack and to continue working.

Ilara meanwhile berated both brothers for failing to keep the evidence hidden. She instructed them not to move the hoodie now that it has already been spotted. 'If you move it, it will raise suspicion. Just keep the door closed at all times. Can you do this simple task?" she demanded firmly. Both boys simply hung their heads in shame and did as asked.

CHAPTER 33

It was midday, and Jack was once again in his well-maintained Mustang. Eighties music was blaring on the radio. He was about to perform an unethical act, something he swore that he'd never do when he was made captain. It would compromise the investigation and his reputation if anyone found out.

The chief turned up at the luxurious house in Sag Harbour. Engine off, on-duty weapons stored in the dashboard. As he got out, he was met with resistance from the resident's guards. 'Cops aren't allowed here,' they said firmly.

'Do you know who I am?' Jack asked proudly.

Before anything could escalate, Stella came out on the balcony above the entrance. 'Play nice boys. Let him in,' she said mischievously.

The two tall men stepped out of his way and gestured that he could go in. Jack simply chuckled and proceeded to enter.

Gina, the maid, opened the door and notified him that Stella would be down in a few minutes. She escorted him into a private office and asked, 'Any drink?'

'No, thanks.'

The servant simply bowed and left the room. He sat down and shut his eyes, in complete silence. Moments passed before the door opened. Jack opened his eyes, only to see the donna in red lingerie. He gasped, maybe a little overwhelmed.

'Like what you see?' Stella asked coyly.

He avoided the subject and got straight to the point. 'Stella, I have to turn the boys in.'

'What are you on about?'

'We may have found some incriminating evidence at the warehouse, the one east of Staten Island.'

'Yeah, I heard your friends paid a visit. They didn't actually have a warrant to search the premises, did they?'

'Stella, it's just a matter of time . . .'

'On what grounds can they search the warehouse?'

'Well, we found the DNA evidence at the crime scene, the cigarette butt.'

'Circumstantial! We own the construction site. I could have easily sent Angelo there to monitor the progress of the project.'

'And what about the car? From the impound lot around the corner.'

'What about it?'

'Security cameras? Don't you think we can catch Angelo on it?'

'Well, did you?'

'Stop bullshitting. You know we will find something sooner or later.'

Both stayed quiet for some time, trying to figure out where to go from there.

Stella knew she could not envision her boys being in jail while she ran her empire. Even though they messed up fairly simple instructions, it was her orders they were following after all. Jack could see the dilemma she was in and offered an alternative.

'Unless you turned yourself in, offered some information on other associates and got immunity for your sons,' he suggested.

She paced around as she pondered for what felt like a lifetime. It was a big sacrifice to make for her family. She could not imagine the rest of her life in jail. However, she smiled sneakily, betting on her previous luck of always getting out of sticky situations. She would come up with a plan later, she promised herself, but she had other things on her mind right now.

Jack watched her all this time and could not help thinking she still had the flame in her. Her deliberate attire aided the thoughts and took Jack to an imaginary place he had promised he wouldn't go when he left his house that evening.

He was lost in his wild thoughts when he suddenly realised that Stella had boldly got onto his lap and had started to kiss him. 'If I'm going to jail, let's have some fun for the last time.'

Having her so close revived the passion that they had shared once upon a time. He could not resist any longer. 'Fuck it. Are the doors locked bella?'

'Of course, *amore*,' she replied softly as they both gave in to temptation.

CHAPTER 34

Early evening had arrived. The birds were singing and crowds fluttered on the streets of Brooklyn. Among the tourist flock, Finn had spent the last fifteen minutes updating his wife-to-be on the phone as he walked.

'I saw the news. Are you sure I can't do anything honey? I can come back?' Gigi suggested.

'No, it's fine. She's sleeping in the guest room in case she needs support or whatever.'

'Are you sure that's a good idea?'

'What do you mean?'

'Come on Finn, we know she wants you.'

There was no way he was going to admit to his fiancée that she was right, that Jessie had come on to him. He spoke quickly, 'Not this again. I can handle her. Gotta go honey.'

'Love you.'

'Love you too, take care of the bump.' He was relieved to end the chat, and just in time as he arrived at his destination. He thought some fresh pizza would cheer up Jessie, but the front door of the legendary pizzeria was closed.

'Hmm, what's going on?' he said to himself, as he could see the lights inside. He went to the back, and as he entered, he saw two familiar figures having a secret meeting.

He felt very confused as Jack and he would always attend off-the-record meetings together. He stepped forward softly and hid in the storeroom, leaving the door ajar so he could listen in without getting noticed.

The smells of fresh dough and the wood oven were afloat. There were three chefs prepping ahead of the dinner service. One pizza was already in the oven for Jack. Pepperoni with extra garlic, as always.

The chief came to this pizzeria all the time when he was young. Now he only visited occasionally, usually to have off-the-radar meetings. His close relationship with the owner enabled him to have privacy by closing the restaurant to the public temporarily when requested.

He was waiting for an acquaintance with whom he had worked on a few cases. Jack liked him because he was easy to manipulate. Plenty of times, he had managed to bend the law a little with some simple influencing. He took a big gulp of soda and then looked out of the window while he waited. After a few minutes, the Brooklyn ADA, Ervin Crocker, arrived. He was a big, stuffy fella with an '80s moustache and a receding hairline.

After a general catch-up, the pizza arrived with some plates and beers. Being the fat ass Ervin was, he dived in straight away, without table manners. He then made a mess, like a child. Jack sighed at the disarray but decided to ignore it.

'Erv, listen, I got a winner on my hands. Big break for you and a headache alleviated for me.'

The lawyer was paying attention but had his mouth full. He simply nodded for Jack to continue.

'You heard about the Mazzolas and the construction murders?'

'Mmmm.'

'The donna wants to confess to the crimes but wants full immunity for her sons, even though they did it.' He went on to tell him the whole story.

Ervin finally finished feasting and got serious. 'That's nearly impossible if she didn't have a huge hand in it.'

'She ordered it, though.'

'Eh, not enough for the two boys that committed the crime. Have you ever seen people get immunity like this?'

'Was hoping this would be a big exception. It is a big fish, after all.'

'Errr, I am not sure.'

'Come on man, we have done good together, let's continue it.'

'I just don't see it happening.'

'Why not? It would be a big coup for the department. Imagine the headlines, "Mob and associates taken down, swept up, the streets are cleaner, etc." . . .'

'Mmm, you know I feel uncomfortable with high stake cases.'

'Bro, I'll be there to support you. Hell, I'll do most of the work, and you can take the credit.'

'It has started to sound appealing to be honest.'

'Why don't you ask your boss? I'll order another pizza for you in the meantime.'

The assistant was just about to be sold. He proceeded to make the phone call to his boss. After some back and forth, he hung up.

'Today is your lucky day. The boss wants the deal at any cost.'

'That's fabulous!'

'Now, where is that pizza?'

Jack signalled the chef to hurry up. He then turned to Ervin and advised him, 'You fat bastard, you need to go on a diet or have the fat sucked out.'

'And miss out on all the deliciousness? Shut the fuck up, nigga.' They both laughed raucously and spent some time reminiscing about old cases before heading to the station to set up necessary arrangements for the next day.

Finn? He was simply shocked. He was having a hard time comprehending what he had just witnessed. He could not have imagined in his wildest dream that his childhood friend would sabotage an investigation for his own personal gain.

However, he was also pleased with his last-minute decision to record the meeting. With the evidence in hand, he was glad to have the leverage he could use later on if needed.

CHAPTER 35

The Mazzola brothers were smartly dressed. Probably the best in Sag Harbour that night. The elder brother was wearing a navy jacket and trousers, dark socks, leather shoes, a black tie and a crisp white shirt. Younger brother? Grey jacket and trousers with black shirt and tie.

They were driving towards the family home. 'You know that the meal will be glorious whenever we dress up,' Luciano commented. Angelo simply nodded in agreement and confirmed, 'It will be a lavish feast.' 'We got to do this more than once a month.'

'I disagree. Having it too often will make the dinner loses its charm.' 'Mmm, perhaps you're right. I just like the idea of having fresh lobsters and caviar every day.' Angelo chuckled at his brother's childish quip.

At the Mazzola mansion, Stella and Ilara were having a moving conversation. 'You don't have to take this on yourself. I have an idea. Remember Finn?'

'Yes, I do, always smelling of alcohol.'

'The other day, I overheard that his fiancée is pregnant.'

'So what?'

'Blackmail, a get-out-of-jail free card for the boys.'

'I'm not following?'

'We can get Finn to make all the evidence disappear.'

'And why will he do that?'

'He will. We'll threaten the safety of his partner and unborn child.'

'But I have already told Jack about my plans. And I am also nervous about all eyes being on the boys. They can fuck up any day, especially Luciano.'

Ilara considered what her mum was saying, slightly annoyed and confused at why her mum would tell Jack before discussing with her first. Nevertheless, it could still work. 'In that case, we'll submit all the necessary evidence to make the law enforcement think we are co-operating toward a plea agreement. Once the evidence is gone, any deal will become invalid as they'll have nothing to charge you with, setting you free. I'll handle all the formalities.'

'Bella, you genius! This is why you should be my number two in our Mazzola empire.'

'No, I want something even better.'

'What could be better than being one of the richest in the country?'

'Freedom.'

'You mean . . .?'

'Yes, I'll be helping the boys one last time. If the plan works, I'm gone. Start a new life somewhere far.'

'But—'

'No buts. I've had enough. A long time ago, I made a promise that the day I'm willing to break the law, I'm walking away, so I don't get rotten any further.'

'OK bella, you win. I suppose Joanna is part of your plans?' enquired Stella. The young lawyer was shocked that her mum knew about the secret relationship, 'How did you know?' 'A mother knows bella,' she said softly. A little kiss on her forehead followed.

Just then, the brothers pulled up outside. As they came through the door, classic piano music was playing. Mouth-watering aromas emerged from the kitchen. Gina came from the wine cellar with one hand holding glasses and champagne in the other. 'Gents, *bevanda?* (drink?)'

Both brothers looked at each other and smiled. The duo grabbed the goblets and waited for the maid to fill them. They both felt that the dinner was going to be luxurious and memorable.

'*Ragazzi!* (Boys!) Come here, please!' A voice came from the dining room. The duo obliged and went through to the freshly decorated space. The table had candles, a recently ironed tablecloth, swan-shaped napkins and shiny cutlery.

They were welcomed by their mum and sister, both lavishly dressed. The women were wearing laced-up corsets, both black. They all sat down and consumed a humongous dinner together as a family.

CHAPTER 36

Somewhere deep in Brooklyn, a couple was having a candle-lit dinner in a small but cosy apartment.

Tom reached across and held Audrey's hand. 'I'm glad we are having some quality time together. Thank you for cooking this delicious meal.' He kissed her hand. She giggled.

'It's the least I can do after you got suspended from work because of me.'

'Well, it was worth it. Anything for you sunshine.'

'Actually, there's one more thing I could have some help with.' She leaned forward, playing with her pink hair, cleavage open and subtly biting her lips.

Tom knew he was in trouble. He wouldn't be able to say no, even if the potential favour was going to be a mammoth task. 'Honey, what is it?'

'Can you give me an update on the case? Have a little look into your fancy police database on the iPad?'

'Audrey...'

'Please babe, it would really mean a lot. There might be a reward for you in this,' she winked.

The suspended PR manager got a little annoyed. 'Are you just using me?'

His partner was a little shocked. They'd been through a lot together, so she felt a little hurt. However, she had been asking a lot of him recently. Holding her tongue, she spoke softly,

'Absolutely not honey, we are a team, we should be helping each other out without questioning,' and looked away sadly.

He knew he had fucked up. Sighing heavily, he opened his device and logged into the police software. After a bit of browsing and scrolling, his eyes widened, and he let out a gasp.

Audrey turned and smiled gently. She knew Tom would come through. 'What is it babe?'

'You won't believe this. Jack is apparently related to Angelo Mazzola!'

'No way!'

'See it for yourself. Look but no scrolling,' Tom handed over the iPad.

She eagerly grabbed the device and spent a couple of minutes scanning the report. This was big, something that could propel her career to new heights. A big break was something she desperately needed at this point in her career. It would make all her hard work and sleepless nights worth it.

Laying the device down, she wanted to show her fiancée some appreciation. 'Ready for your gift mister?' she flirted, grabbed his hand and led him to the bedroom.

'You betcha!' Tom responded excitedly, and both laughed as if they were teens once again.

CHAPTER 37

A gentle breeze filled the air during the journey between the Mazzola mansion at Sag Harbour and the Brooklyn police station, with a brief stop at the warehouse midway. The limo window was slightly ajar and the fresh air was a welcome distraction. There was soft jazz music in the background to calm the mood.

'Are you sure about this?' Stella cautiously asked her daughter again. She was referring to the plan cooked up the previous night.

'Yes, I'm certain it'll work. You should've seen how thrilled Finn was when he found out. Having a family is clearly very important to him.'

'Bella, I'm so proud of you. You are the rightful heir to the throne.'

'No way, I need to get out of New York. Sick and tired of the whole family business.'

'But Bella . . .'

'No, my decision is final. I can't wait to build a new life in Maldives,' Ilara asserted her vision.

As they arrived, they noticed the crowds around the station, mostly press. Amongst them was a very anxious Audrey. This was a big segment, currently the main feature on national news cable. It was a make-or-break opportunity for her. 'Get the camera ready! Start rolling!' she ordered the meek cameraman, who was clumsily trying to set it all up. When it was finally live, she gave a summary of the developments thus far.

Stella softly asked her two tall and buff men to clear the way. Both got out immediately. 'Move please,' the two bodyguards requested firmly. The paparazzi ignored them and continued to encircle the luxury vehicle. The well-dressed guardians simply sighed and raised their voices. 'Get out of our way, you cockroaches!' The crowd dispersed but only partially.

Jack and Ervin had arrived to escort them in. Multiple flashes went off as Stella stepped out of her limo, followed by Ilara. Press vultures were shouting out all sorts of questions. PR training kicked in for the lawyer, who repeatedly answered, 'No comment.'

But one question stood out, bringing all sorts of mixed expressions to the faces. 'Ms Mazzola, is it true that one of your sons is related to the chief of this police station?'

Before the donna could respond, Jack stepped in, bristling with annoyance and anger at another leak. He managed to dodge the question skilfully and walked away, 'No further comment.'

The influence that the media had on the outcomes of criminal cases had bothered him for a long time. It was time for a crackdown, he decided, and Tom needed to go after this latest betrayal.

Audrey was a little taken aback but kept calm and continued to give the latest on the case to the camera. Though not as expected, it wasn't a total bust, she thought. She managed to facetime on live TV and put out her best. She decided to worry about Tom later.

Once the guests were cleared of the security protocols at the entrance, the four headed to the interrogation room. Before entering, the chief excused himself for a moment, then speed-dialled the PR manager.

'Yes, boss?' Tom answered.

'You leaked again, you bum?' Jack asked furiously. Tom stuttered, which was his tell.

'Fuck's sake, Thomas. You know what? You are relieved of your duties. Your stuff will be sent home, all police privileges are revoked. Do not come here again.'

'But —'

'No buts. Fuck off now.' The chief brushed him off, took a deep breath and returned to the group.

CHAPTER 38

A jaunty tune rang. As Jack reached for his phone again, everyone stared at him, raising their eyebrows at the childish theme song. The chief ignored the looks, gestured them to go inside and answered the call. 'Yes honey?'

His eldest daughter was on the other end. 'Dad, what are they saying? Is it true that you are —'

Jack cut her off before she could continue. 'Darling, don't listen to the news. I will explain everything later, I promise.'

'But Dad —'

'Grace, I have to go now. Make sure Liz takes her medicine please,' he ordered firmly before hanging up, leaving his kid with more questions than answers. He ran his hand over his shiny scalp before taking a deep breath and entering the interview room.

All lights were switched on. Windows were slightly ajar. Ice-cold water bottles sat waiting on the table and cigar smoke filled the air. Pens and papers were ready. The camera was on and the red light started to flash, indicating that the recording was in progress.

'Today is 1st of June 2020, 2 p.m. This is Brooklyn ADA Ervin Haynes. Ladies and gent, please state your full names.'

'Chief Jack Feltham, Brooklyn Homicide Department,' he said, with a cigar in his hand.

'Stella Mazzola, CEO of the Mazzola Co.'

'Ilara Mazzola, representing Mazzola Co.'

Ervin settled his suit for the hundredth time today. He was a submissive dimwit who was clearly enjoying his authority a little too much as he was holding the cards for the first time in his life. This was probably his big break. The chubby fella wanted to make the jump to the big league, being his own DA, not pandering to his boss, and being respected by other high-ranking lawyers. Maybe even open his own firm one day.

'So, we are here to make a deal regarding the murders of Craig Turner and Jordi Knowles.'

Stella spoke up and demanded immunity for her two boys. She got straight to the point, super direct. Ervin shuffled in his chair as he became a little uncomfortable. He never liked it when a female asserted herself boldly or dominated a conversation, a misogynist at heart, some might argue. Jack noticed, cleared his throat and nudged his colleague to encourage him.

'Stella, any information you give us will have to be certified by the investigative team. Terms will be granted only if the info is accurate.'

CHAPTER 39

Stella obviously ordered the crime but did not pull the trigger. After a bit of storytelling, both men were taken aback with what they had just heard. Even with the reveal, Ervin had to corroborate some of the evidence that was found.

'OK Stella, this is a lot to process. We have to ask some questions to verify the claims.'

She ignored the sweaty attorney and turned her attention to her former lover. The strawberry blonde twirled her hair and brazenly asked, 'Jacky boy, aren't you going to take charge? You know I like it when you do.' Both Ilara and Ervin gulped.

Jack ignored the flirt and tapped his cigar on the mini ashtray. He then leaned forward and started the enquires. 'I assume you wanted Craig out of the way for monetary gain?'

'Yes sir.'

Jack took the weapon out of the sealed evidence bag and slammed it on the table. 'Recognise it?' he questioned.

'Yes I do, I told the boys to take it. Told them to wear gloves so it can't be traced back to them. Of course, they didn't listen.'

'The girl?'

'A tragedy. Wrong place, wrong time.'

'The car?'

'We took it from the impound lot round the corner from the warehouse. VIN number noted on the paperwork. Angelo tried to make it look like a hit and run. After the shooting, Luca went to the safehouse near Bath Beach.'

'That explains the camera shot of him,' Ervin mused. 'I assume one of your sons smokes?'

'Angelo does.'

'That puts him at the scene of the crime.'

Stella then reached into her huge bag and took out the blood-stained hoodie (that was also seen on the camera and in the warehouse office) along with a size 10 boot, matching the boot prints found at the scene of the crime. Jack called out to Jasmine, who was watching from behind the mirrors. She quickly came in and bagged the evidence before taking it to the lab to process.

After a few more questions about other associates that the donna had critical information on, Ilara interrupted to get assurances on the deal. 'I assume you are going to validate the story and get back to us?'

'Under normal circumstances, yes, but after listening to what has been said in the past hour, we can start the paperwork and get it all sorted within the next few hours.'

Ilara insisted that the family needed a couple of days to get their affairs in order. But Stella disagreed and requested that she be escorted through the back door to avoid the media.

The two men exited the room to get started on due diligence. Ilara opened her briefcase and started preparing the necessary documents. Stella? She gently nudged her daughter to get confirmation that the plan was progressing nicely. Her offspring simply nodded back to confirm it was proceeding as expected.

Meanwhile, Jessie was in the mortuary collecting her sister's body. She was having a hard time controlling her emotions. But it would have been worse if Finn hadn't been there to support her.

CHAPTER 40

It was past midnight and Finn was walking briskly towards home. He had just finished helping Jessie set up the wake service, which was going to take place within the next couple of days. 'I'm going to have nightmares tonight after seeing Jordi's coffin,' he muttered to himself.

The phone rang. Finn saw an 'unknown number' titled on the screen. *Who on earth would be calling at this time?* he wondered.

'Hello Mr Kingsley, I hope you are well.'

Finn instantly recognised the voice on the other end as his courtroom adversary Ilara. He had not won against her even once in the five battles they partook against each other. She always pulled a rabbit out of the hat at the very last second, causing him to lose each time.

Skipping the pleasantries, he asked, 'What do you want?'

'No manners eh?'

'Not for you.'

'Rude. Anyway, just wanted to congratulate you again.'

'You didn't call me for that.'

'Smart boy. It would be a shame if your partner were to suddenly have a miscarriage.'

'What?'

'Relax, just a hypothetical.'

'You —'

'You will have a beautiful family, I'm sure of it. But only if the evidence due to be submitted tomorrow suddenly vanishes.'

'Are you blackmailing me?'

'Honey, how about thinking of this enlightening convo as a business deal.'

'Why are you doing this? You're no better than others in your family.'

'For freedom! I think you now understand the severity of the situation. I trust you'll make the right choice, and yes, I'm calling from a burner. Goodbye, Mr Kingsley.'

'Ilara!!!' Finn screamed. He tapped the screen a few times in disbelief. He stumbled onto the nearest bench and took a few moments to collect himself. He knew he had to protect his expanding family at any cost. Finn looked up at the Brooklyn Bridge skyline, and an idea came to him. He picked up his mobile again and phoned Jack.

'Bro, I have a problem.'

'It's late, can we do this tomorrow?'

'No, where are you?'

'Office, about to head home.'

Finn went on to explain what had just happened in the past few minutes.

'Damn Finn, I don't know whether to propose a toast to you and Gigi or get some security over to her.'

'Destroy the evidence please.'

'What the fuck, dude? Have you lost your damn mind?'

'Funny, I was going to ask the same thing of you.'

'Huh?'

'I know about the meeting in the diner. Bet you visited Stella to set the interview in motion. How would it look to the bosses upstairs if they see you abusing your authority for newfound relations?'

Silence was adrift and the air was filled with tension. Both men were contemplating the next steps.

'OK look, leave it with me, I'll handle it. The evidence will be no more.'

'How?'

'I'll dump it in the fucking river, what else?'

'Thank you Jack. This would benefit both of us.'

'This discussion never happened.'

'What discussion?'

'Fuck off now.' Jack hung up. Finn set the phone down, ran his hand through his hair and took a sip from the flask, which was hidden in his jacket pocket. He then threw the drink away, promising himself to stop drinking from this moment, for the sake of his family.

CHAPTER 41

The court was filled with paparazzi waiting eagerly to take pictures. Both victims' families were seated on the left side, while the defendant's supporters sat on the right. As the courtroom doors opened, Stella came out in handcuffs. She was ushered through the crowd with the help of the bailiffs. Cheers and jeers grew loud as the room got chaotic. Donna lifted her hand as a way of thanking her supporters. This only escalated the noise on the left.

Judge Taylor entered the space and sat down. He had to bang his gavel and remind everyone to be quiet, adding that he would be more than happy to dish out contempt of court charges if anyone didn't behave. The court attendees finally calmed down so the proceedings could start.

While the case introductions and formalities took place, Jack quietly entered the courtroom and advanced softly to sit behind the prosecution bench with his colleagues. After Judge Taylor finished droning on, he asked the prosecutor Ervin Crocker, 'I understand that we have a plea agreed?'

Ervin got up and wiped away the sweat on his forehead. 'Yes your honour,' he said nervously.

'Please state the details of the agreed plea for the court,' the judge ordered.

Before the attorney could announce the stipulation, Jack spotted an opportunity to disrupt the case. He stood up and leaned forward, whispering just loud enough for Jessie to hear, 'Ervin, we have a problem.'

'Not the right time Jack,' Ervin clenched his teeth and hissed back.

'Dude, the evidence has gone missing.'

'The fuck are you on about?'

Judge Taylor was losing his patience and curtly interjected, 'Mr Crocker, is this the right time for you to chat with your mates? Please enlighten us, what could be more important right now?'

The Brooklyn ADA gulped and answered sheepishly, 'Apologies your honour, it seems that the necessary evidence has vanished.'

Suddenly, a roar was heard from the left side, barring Finn. Jessie could not contain herself and spoke out of place. 'Evidence gone missing? How convenient. This is bullshit. The perps will continue with their lives as if nothing happened. How is that justice for the dead, for my sister?' she bellowed from the top of her lungs.

She then charged towards the Mazzola brothers, spitting out all sorts of indecent phrases and accusing them of evidence tampering.

The judge didn't like what he was seeing but was sympathetic. 'Detective Knowles, I understand that you are hurting, but you have to calm down,' he advised. However, before he could continue, Jessie challenged him. 'Or what? Throw me in jail for speaking the truth?'

'Don't try me Miss,' he responded with authority.

Before she could reply, Finn apologised on her behalf and dragged her out of the courtroom.

Ilara then stood up from the defence bench and attempted to apply the 'dismiss the case' motion. 'Since there is no evidence that my client has committed this heinous crime, I move to dismiss the case. This was a witch hunt from the beginning.'

Ervin tried to counter, 'Well, hang on, Miss —' but could not continue as he was stopped by the judge. 'You are not getting the case dismissed so easily Miss Mazzola. The prosecution and the defence wouldn't have brought this plea agreement forward if there was no evidence in the first place. Mr Crocker, you have 48 hours to recover the evidence, otherwise I'll have to grant the defence's motion. Understood?'

Both teams agreed in unison before the judge adjourned the court. The Mazzola mother and daughter duo quietly congratulated each other, in the knowledge that the plan had worked.

Ilara felt she was finally free from the stressful life she lead, mostly representing the family. Next step, life by the sea with her lover!

CHAPTER 42

It was very late at night. The funeral service and wake took place a few hours ago. The house was empty apart from a newly solitary inhabitant. Jessie was once again on the piano.

Everything seemed to be falling apart. The case against the Mazzola family had collapsed, and all of them were roaming free, while she had a big hole in her heart. Justice for her late sister had not been served.

Despite the soothing tunes cutting through the tension in the room, Jess was struggling to cope with the emotional pain. It felt as raw today as it did on the day she got the dreadful news. She couldn't let this go, even though she had tried. And then, just like that, she abruptly decided to break the oath she had once made at the police academy. 'I'm ending this.'

Bing. She opened her mobile and rang Jasmine, 'Hey Jazzy, can you ping me Luciano's location please?'

'Why?'

'I have a theory,' she lied.

'You can't be getting involved, even though it is difficult not to. I could also get into serious trouble. Besides, the case is over.'

'I can get him on something else. Please Jaz, I'm going mad here!' Jess wailed desperately.

'But . . .' The junior detective was torn between two options: to help her colleague or to follow policy.

'Please!'

'On the condition that you let Finn know.'

'Yeah yeah, sure,' she said hastily.

In just a minute, the junior detective had notified Jess of ongoing activities at Coney Island.

'Thanks Jaz, I owe you big time.'

'You are phoning Finn, yes?' Jasmine was concerned that Jess was about to go off the rails.

'I'm with him at the moment. Thanks again,' she fibbed once again and hung up. Finn was out getting some old-fashioned Chinese takeaway.

She picked up her off-duty gun, put her jacket on and headed out of Finn's house. Her *iPhone* was purposely left behind as she did not want anyone contacting or tracing her. The car engine hummed loudly as it was turned on. A few seconds later, she was on her way to do the unimaginable.

In her mind, Jessie was running through all her good and bad memories of Jordi. The twenty minute journey to Coney Island was an emotional rollercoaster. She got out of her car and opened her trunk. Bullet vest on, a silenced pistol and some spare clips were packed.

CHAPTER 43

Some few miles away, Jasmine was a nervous wreck. She had a gut feeling that Jess was up to no good. After a bit of pacing back and forth, the junior detective decided to call Finn.

'Finn, is Jessie with you?' she questioned eagerly.

'No.'

'That's what I thought, I'm afraid!' she bemoaned.

'Huh, what do you mean?' the confused ADA said. He had had a long day and was revising the case notes alongside the empty takeaway containers.

'She phoned me a while ago asking for the location of the brothers, and now I think . . .'

'Where?'

'Coney Island.'

'Thanks for telling me. Don't tell anyone else, especially Jack, please.' He hung up and rushed out of the door. Finn was afraid of the worst possible outcome.

Jasmine was relieved that she had shared the latest development with Finn, only to be shocked as her boss crept up behind her.

'What did Finn not want me to know?'

'Errm . . .'

'Jasmine, do you like your job?' he asked ominously.

'Yes . . .'

'It would be a shame if you threw away your career on account of some alcoholic,' he said firmly.

The junior detective was taken aback by her boss's threatening demeanour. She didn't want things to escalate further, so she gave in and told him what had happened in the past few hours.

CHAPTER 44

It was four in the morning and the whole theme park was absolutely drenched in torrential rain. But the lights were illuminated all around and delivery vehicles were scattered. Music was blaring, indicating some human presence at the famed Coney Island fairground.

Jessie strolled quietly through the car park. As she spotted a guard at the entrance, she took cover behind a van. The security felt light. She took a moment to think. *Should I hold the guard hostage and demand to see the Mazzola brothers? Or take a stealthy approach?*

She decided on the latter. The bouncer was enormous, and a submachine gun was visible in his holster. It was vital not to draw attention, she thought as she attempted to navigate through the car park.

She knew some real shit was about to go down. After a quick prayer, she took aim at the guard from behind the van. Luckily, the lookout wasn't paying attention. Jessie took a deep breath and squeezed the trigger. Splat! The first sentry went down with a hole in his head.

She started to shake at the realisation that she was now a cold-blooded killer. The perp knelt next to the body, trying to push away the echoes of her sister screaming, 'Don't throw your life away!'

A new song started to play over the speakers, bringing Jessie back down to earth. She took a few minutes to collect herself. She grabbed her flask, filled with 'Dutch courage' to increase her bravery, before going into the battle. She hoped it would also help her to stay calm during whatever would be the aftermath.

She then hid the body in the ticket booth and took the guard's gun. 'You won't be needing that!' Jessie chortled. A bigger magazine and a faster rate of fire could prove to be useful. She turned the safety pin off before making her way into the theme park.

CHAPTER 45

The first area she came across was the toilets and gift shops square. There were two sentries out in the open, shooting the breeze. They were conversing about the recent sports news. Jessie once again took shelter, this time behind an information board.

POP! POP! The weapon fired. The first guard went down like a sack of potatoes. His partner became alert, but before he could figure out where the bullets were fired from, another POP! POP! went off, killing him on the spot. A pool of blood started to form and mix with the puddle on the concrete.

The rogue detective broke cover and went to the bodies to check if they were alive or dead. As she confirmed they were gone, her confidence grew. Suddenly, a shout for help was heard, coming from the gift shop. 'Hey guys, bring in more boxes,' an employee of the crime syndicate asked his colleagues, not knowing they were dead. 'Damn! Should've reconned first,' she whispered to herself. Quickly and stealthily jogging over, she took cover behind the exit door of the gift shop.

'These drugs aren't gonna carry themselves guys, turn the music off, it's too loud!' the fella inside the gift shop complained. No response. 'Lazy bastards!' he muttered, before going out to collect the packages himself. As the drug operative exited the store, he was stopped in his tracks. He felt the cold and wet barrel of the gun pressed against his temple.

'Hey there,' Jessie smirked. A disgusting, pungent smell of ammonia suddenly filled the air. She sniffed, only to realise the fella had pissed himself. 'Ah, come on dude!' The poor man was trembling, in obvious fear for his life.

'Are you going to answer my questions?' Jessie asked firmly.

He simply nodded, hoping this living nightmare would be over soon.

'Good, that was easy. Now, how many of you are here?'

'Eleven.'

'Including the brothers?'

'No.'

'Where are they?'

'I'm not sure.'

The rogue detective was losing patience. She cocked the pistol to remind him about what was at stake. 'Try again, mister.'

'They sometimes like to hang out at the haunted house. Now please let me go! I won't call the cavalry, I swear,' he sobbed.

'Sorry, I can't let you go,' she said coldly before pressing the trigger, and down he went. Blood splattered all over her vest but she did not give a toss. The vicious killer moved on to the bumper car arena.

CHAPTER 46

Cars were spread around. It was difficult to navigate through the mess in the dark. But the lights started to flash from the go-kart track, which had a generic eight shape with a bridge. She was relieved for a bit of guidance and took shelter behind a blue car located between the railings and the exit. Jessie took a quick look at the tracks and spotted two joyriders. She also saw a guard in the control shed.

She scanned the area one more time to avoid any potential shootout before breaking cover. She mounted using the back of the bumper car and aimed. A loud burst of gunshots rang in her ears as she fired at the stationary sentry inside the shack. Glass shattered and blood splashed all over the shed.

The guards on the kart missed the noise amid the deafening music. This helped Jessie to calmly move her line of sight to the mini roadways and shoot at the red kart that just went around the bend. The female driver lost control as the bullets went through her left shoulder. The small but hefty vehicle crashed into the pit stop hut. It tipped over, and the shelf containing heavy repair equipment fell on the driver, killing her instantly.

Her partner suddenly became alert and spotted the rogue detective. He became enraged and shouted, 'You are so fucking dead!' The fella stepped up a gear, drove up the bridge and smashed through the barriers in order to fly through the air. The flying kart was heading straight for Jessie. The submachine gun stopped firing. It took a couple of seconds for her to comprehend that the magazine was finished.

She could not believe the fearlessness of her oncoming attacker. She dodged and briefly lay on her belly down on the arena to avoid the oncoming wheel of death. She then spun around onto her back, grabbed her pistol and blasted a few rounds. A couple hit him beneath the shoulder blades, and one penetrated the fuel tank.

The kart landed awkwardly on top of a couple of bumper cars, and suddenly, the whole pile was engulfed in flames. Screams of agony would have been heard for miles but were covered by the loudspeakers nearby. Both crashes were a sight to behold. Jessie took a moment to catch her breath. But soon heard noises from the other lookouts who saw the flames and decided to make a dash towards it.

CHAPTER 47

The rogue detective approached the famed boardwalk, saw a couple of attentive guards and immediately took cover behind a bench. However, in doing so, she slipped while attempting to reload. She dropped her back-up pistol, which went off and gave away her position.

'Damn, that bitch is here!' the enemy screeched into the speakers to notify others. Both sentries started to fire blindly into open space while trying to find cover. Jessie had to duck a few times to avoid the onslaught of bullets.

She waited for the shooters to reload so she could fire back. 'Click', she heard. Now was the time. Jessie peeked and shot. A few bursts and the guy behind the counter inside the donut store went down as the rounds tore through his chest.

Jessie then turned her line of sight to the candyfloss cart. As she did, her body shook backwards, giving rise to an excruciating pain. She bent down to figure out where the abrupt agony was coming from. Checked the legs, lower abdomen, stomach - there was a lot of blood but no hole. She moved her hand upwards and found the circular cut in the ribcage area. But the wound was through and through, and the bullet had left her body.

Blood began to drip onto the wooden floor and breathing started to become a struggle. But she had to continue fighting despite the ache. *Can't let all this effort go to waste*, she thought to herself.

The other guard repositioned himself, now behind the counter in a jet ski rental kiosk. Jessie took notice of the footsteps and fired. Missed. The enemy fired back, same result.

She counted to five and got up, charged and shot at the same time. This was risky as she was exposed but a success nevertheless as the adversary fell and died instantly. The injured went into the store to hide. She needed time to apply first aid to the lacerations before stumbling on to the next area.

CHAPTER 48

Jessie skipped past the arcade and stopped within a small space occupied by cheesy stall games. Suddenly, her vision started to blur and a flashback ensued. She could visualise herself and her sister running around, trying out different ways to earn fluffy rewards. After a few attempts, there was no prize to take home. 'J, we can't get anything, I suck at these games,' Jordi sulked.

'No you don't, these booths are rigged. These fellas dangle the shiny stuff in front of your eyes. You can spend a lot trying to get second-rate shit to take home. It's a never-ending loop.'

'You are so smart, J, you should be a professor!'

'Nah, I wanna be a detective!'

'Why?'

'Too much injustice in this world, gotta correct some, innit?'

'What if something happens to you or me?'

Jessie took a deep breath, stared into her younger sibling's eyes and cupped her cheeks. 'I won't let anything happen to you, and I'll be careful too.'

'Pinky promise?'

The older sister took a glance at one last stall they hadn't tried. 'Hold on.' She walked over, paid two dollars and took aim with the water gun. Jessie had to knock down three moving bottles with five shots. DING, DING and DING! Easy peasy. The old stall cashier was shocked. She pointed at a large pink teddy bear, and he obliged.

She went back to Jordi and handed over the toy. 'Pinky!'

'Thank you!!! I love you much!' her sister squealed and excitedly hugged back.

'Me too honey!'

A nearby rollercoaster roared WHOOSH! as the cars dipped, bringing Jessie back to reality, the world of real guns. It was strange that the ride was on at this time, so she went to the next stage of her revenge to investigate.

CHAPTER 49

As Jessie limped due to bleeding profusely, a huge red structure came into view. The Wheel of Doom was Coney Island's most attractive attraction. It featured five loops, the usual big dip at the start, a little slant through the haunted house and a splash at the very end of the thrill. It would take a huge ball of steel to weather the storm this rollercoaster would present.

The vengeance seeker blocked her agony and walked through a tunnel entrance before taking cover. This time it was behind the disabled lift doors next to the tracks. She took some deep breaths to contain the pain emitting from her ribcage. She then peeked around the corner, only for a red mist of anger to suddenly appear over her face. She had spotted one of her targets, a certain brown-haired fella. He was preoccupied with controlling the mini carriages.

'OK pricks, one more time, then we gotta get back to work,' Luciano chuckled. He had no idea that the next half an hour would be the last stretch of his life. The automated announcement rang over the speakers, 'Hello ladies and gents, buckle in and hold tight - welcome to the Wheel of Doom!' The two guards hollered loudly in anticipation of what was to come.

It would have been ideal if the guards disappeared and Jessie could have time alone with one half of the Mazzola brothers. However, the ride would have been too short for Jessie. She wanted to take as much time tormenting Luciano as possible. POP! POP! POP! the weapon fired. The first sentry slumped down onto the safety bars. The mini car then proceeded to move out of the platform and ascend the tracks.

The second jumped out just in time and ducked behind the power room. Luciano, being the wimp that he was, left his colleague to do the dirty work and escaped into the haunted house. 'Get back here, you little shit!' Jessie demanded.

'Kiss my ass, *puttana*! (bitch!)' Luciano squeaked as he ran away into the haunted house.

She tried to chase after him but was met with a torrent of bullets fired by the second goon. As Jessie sought to take cover, she spotted a switch-box above the enemy. She shot the fuse; an electrical spark went off and electrocuted him partially. He fell onto the coaster path, only to be hit by a second set of cars, killing the fella on impact.

Jessie was starting to get overwhelmed with the bloodbath she had inflicted upon the park, but the job was nearly done.

CHAPTER 50

The haunted house hosted the last battle of this personal war. It was shaped like a mini castle. Smoke blowing out of the chimney, ghost posters all over the front and a cheesy, partially functioning neon sign welcomed Jessie. She cautiously approached the door and tried to pry it open. She grunted and flinched as she pushed and pulled until it finally opened with a loud creak.

'HAHAHAHAHA,' a mechanical skeleton bellowed and lunged at Jessie. It shook her briefly, but she managed to hold her nerves. The siblings used to visit this attraction often when they were young, so she remembered the layout vaguely. She proceeded to the grid-like graveyard, leaving a trail of blood drops.

Jessie had to be careful. Some of the fake graves and tombstones had robotic zombies that would jump out if stepped on. She had forgotten which slots were empty and which ones were full. She took a drawn-out deep breath and decided to move ahead apprehensively.

After a bit of hopping and skipping, managing to avoid most jump scares, she finally reached the annex where the rollercoaster intersected with the haunted house. Jessie heard footsteps and looked ahead, detecting Luciano once again. She burst through the door and aimed, only to be caught off-guard by the older brother.

'Hello Jessie, we meet again,' Angelo announced menacingly. He cocked his revolver and pressed the barrel to the back of her head. 'Drop it and slide the piece over to Luca.'

She had no choice and did what was asked of her. The gun slid over to Luciano, who picked it up and turned the safety pin on. 'Damn girl, you shouldn't have come after us. This is a war you were never going to win,' the ginger one laughed.

'You son of a bitch. Jordi was the pride and joy of my life. You took her away,' Jessie trembled.

The killer spoke up and apologised. 'She was at the wrong place, wrong time. The gun went off. I never meant to kill her.'

Angelo sighed and told his brother to shut up. He continued, 'Ignore him, he's a useless shit. Anyway, you aren't any better than us. Look at the destruction you've caused tonight. Aww, you're bleeding.' He pressed the wound deliberately to inflict pain. Jessie flinched and cursed him under her breath.

'That must be hurting like hell. It is an absolute shame that it won't be looked at. Doesn't matter, no rescue needed, you're joining your sister anyway, *veni, vidi, vici!*'

Jessie closed her eyes and counted to five. She then smirked as a rumbling noise came upon them, and the rollercoaster once again thundered above Angelo. 'Wrong fool, not on my watch!' Jessie proclaimed brashly.

Making the best use of the split-second distraction, she spun around, disarmed Angelo and shot him with his own weapon. There was a brand-new hole between his eyes as he went down. The gun then jammed.

'NOOOOOOOO!' Luciano screamed and scrambled to use the confiscated gun. Jessie turned 180 degrees, grabbed her knife from her belt and threw it at her main adversary.

PLOP! The sharp blade embedded into his heart. He clutched his chest before falling down and bleeding out.

CHAPTER 51

As she exited the haunted house, she came upon the legendary Ferris wheel. She and her sister had enjoyed the ride so many times. She vividly remembered that one time when both girls had promised to always look after each over a binge of candyfloss.

Jessie came back to the present day as the sun started to rise. She crumbled to the ground within the wheel pod, thinking she had not kept her promise. The rogue detective tried to take it all in as it had been a hell of a night.

Suddenly, a familiar face burst through the cart gates and crouched against the seats.

'I had to do it Jack. The pain was too much,' Jessie spoke softly.

'You killed my son!' Jack bellowed and stood up quickly.

'They killed my sister!' she shouted back.

Her chief started to shake. He then lifted his gun and aimed at her. 'I'm sorry.' Tears streamed down his face.

'I wouldn't shoot just yet. We should talk,' Finn announced as he arrived just in time, pressing the gun to the back of Jack's head.

'Your timing is impeccable.' The chief wiped away his tears and produced a dry chuckle. 'Do you think you've got the upper hand here, Finn?'

'Well, yeah.'

'Does Jessie know how the evidence went missing? Or should I enlighten her?' Jack said frostily as he turned around, facing his former partner in crime.

It took a couple of moments for Jessie to put the puzzle pieces together, but when she did, she started to tremble. How could her best friend do such a thing and sabotage the case? Not wanting to believe the revelation, she looked into the lawyer's eyes and asked shakily, 'Finn, what is he talking about?'

'Go on, tell her it was for your unborn child,' Jack prodded icily.

Finn knew the cat was out of the bag, and he had nowhere to turn to. He had to do the unthinkable and squeeze the trigger.

POP!

Jack's lifeless body fell face down on the metal floor, drenched in blood. But it didn't feel like the ordeal was over yet. Finn had a cold aura emitting from him as he paced back and forth.

The penny dropped for him as he realised he had killed his childhood friend. All the plans they had made together, gone in a flash. His addiction combined with the stress of the past few weeks had got the better of him. He was not in the right state of mind. And in the same daze, he turned abruptly and aimed at Jessie.

'J, it was either you or my sweet Gigi and our child. I'm sorry,' he whimpered, before squeezing the trigger. Jessie couldn't believe what was happening. BOOM! The gun went off, and red liquid splattered all over the seat as she slumped down.

Finn exited the ride and stumbled to the nearby beach. Once he reached the edge of the tide, he sat down. Realising that the gun was still in his hand, he stared at it for a moment. It felt heavier as it had taken two lives which were both so dear to him. He then dropped the piece to the side.

He looked down to his bloodstained hands, shaking. He ran them through his hair, now red. The lawyer sat for a few minutes, alternating his gaze between the gun and the deep blue sea. He lay down on the sand, not caring about getting wet as the tide brushed against his body, and the water turned red. He attempted to process the massacre that had just taken place at the famed Coney Island.

FINITA

"F INN!" Jessie screamed as she woke up. She had sweat all over her body and she was trembling. It was a horrendous nightmare.

Beautiful piano notes emitted from across the room, encapsulating the air. Jessie remembered that she had fallen asleep on the sofa, due to exhaustion from the previous night's shift.

After a few seconds of getting accustomed to her surroundings, she rushed to her younger sibling. Jordi had stopped playing to probe the sudden noise, only to see Jessie grabbing her for a hug.

"What's going on J?"

"Are you OK Jordi?"

"Yes I am, what's wrong with you?"

"Jesus Christ J, what the fuck?" Finn was both annoyed, at his sleep being interrupted, and alarmed at the sudden noise. He wondered what the commotion was downstairs, so he went to explore.

Rubbing his eyes as he entered the living room, Finn realised that his fiancée Jessie was shaking. "What is the matter honey, are you OK? What happened?" He then reached over and embraced her, slowly stroking her hair. Gently kissing her forehead to calm her down, he asked again. "What happened babe?"

She tried to explain but couldn't get a hold of herself. She attempted to recount the blood, sweat, tears and all she came across in the reverie. The whole saga felt so vivid, to the point it became too much to handle and she started to sob. Both Finn & Jordi cowered over her and cuddled. Her young sister spoke with wisdom, "You're OK honey, it was just a dream."

Story Terrace

Printed in Great Britain
by Amazon